The Attic

Also by Edna Taylor and published by Ginninderra Press
The Skeleton in the Cupboard
Brief Encounters

Edna Taylor

The Attic
& other stories

The Attic & other stories
ISBN 978 1 76041 415 3
Copyright © Edna Taylor 2017

First published 2017 by
GINNINDERRA PRESS
PO Box 3461 Port Adelaide 5015
www.ginninderrapress.com.au

Contents

Abstract

Lucinda liked to visit garage sales on the weekend to hunt for picture frames, which were getting too expensive to buy new. Some of the old discarded pictures had good frames, however, and with a little repair and polish they came up really well.

Lucinda liked to paint landscapes – traditional scenes in oils and watercolours, that were in her opinion, greatly enhanced when surrounded by a nice frame, rather than displayed in an unmounted block canvas, as was becoming more fashionable but also, in Lucinda's opinion, very unattractive.

She parked the car and followed the balloons leading towards the driveway of a big old house; MANOR PLACE, it said on the gate.

It must be a deceased estate, she thought, as she gazed in amazement at the piles of stuff which looked like the entire contents of someone's household.

'Everything must go,' shouted a large gentleman in a bowler hat. 'Any offer considered.'

Quite a few people had already arrived even though it was only nine a.m. and they were delving excitedly into the array of items. There were tables displaying knick-knacks, kitchenware, books and so on, plus furniture and other paraphernalia spread all over the grassy lawns.

Lucinda had learned to be careful at garage sales. It was so easy to buy something on the spur of the moment because it was a bargain and inevitably completely useless. She was now single-minded and only looked for something she needed, which today was picture frames.

Carefully she made her way through the bargain hunters, stepping over items on the ground until she spied what she was looking for.

'Ah, there you are,' she murmured. A stack of old pictures away at the back and to which luckily no one was paying much attention.

She examined them one by one. There were about a dozen. Some of the frames were in poor condition and the old-fashioned printed portraits were very faded. But there were some good frames which she thought would be excellent.

She finally settled on four. Two were about the size she was looking for and two were a little larger. They were good frames, not too ornate and just right for what she had in mind. The pictures they contained were not, in Lucinda's opinion, much good at all. Two were old, poorly executed watercolours of flowers, one with cracked glass; one was a sunset done in acrylics which had faded over the years; and the fourth one was an abstract which she thought was absolutely dreadful. The colours clashed and it was, in her opinion, quite ugly and she wondered how anyone could paint such an atrocity. The frame on that one was the best, though, so she was happy.

Lucinda was feeling very pleased with herself when she took the pictures over to the man who was collecting the money.

'How much are these?' she asked him.

He gave them a cursory glance. 'Ten bucks each, OK?'

He looked at her over his glasses, eyebrows raised expecting her to try and bargain but, 'OK, that's fine, thank you,' she said, and quickly produced forty dollars before he could change his mind. Then she headed off home.

It didn't take long to rip the old pictures from the frames and then she tried her paintings for size. Two were a perfect fit and the teak frame which had been on the abstract looked stunning on her oil painting of the old pioneer cottage. It harmonised beautifully with the brown tones in her picture.

Lucinda took another look at the discarded abstract again. It had been painted on a canvas board in bright primary colours. She turned it upside down and sideways. 'What rubbish,' she muttered. At the bottom was written 'Mountain Morning' in small letters, but the name of the artist was fairly indistinct. She could make out Edward, but the other word was undecipherable. 'Well, Edward,' she said, 'I'm sorry but you're being binned,' and she threw it into the recycling bin with the others for next day's collection.

It wasn't until a week later that Lucinda picked up the local newspaper. A small brochure was enclosed, advertising the forthcoming auction of goods from the estate of Harold Dobbs of Manor Place, who had passed away after a short illness.

It seemed he had been a widower with no family left and had willed everything to the local hospice. Also, he had some valuable antiques and items of value which were to be auctioned The remainder of the household goods had already been sold at a garden sale which had raised nearly $10,000.

Lucinda read on with interest – everything was very expensive – and then she looked at coloured photos of the things to be auctioned. She scanned through quickly, then turned a page back, peering closely at the photo of some of the paintings. There were four in a group. Abstract oil paintings by Edward Abworthy, it said, Mountain Mist, Mountain Morning, Mountain Sunset and Mountain Moonrise. Valued at $25,000 each.

Lucinda couldn't breathe. She went cold, her heart beating so fast she thought she would pass out. Then she sat down for a moment, got herself together and, still feeling shaky, found the phone number of the auctioneers.

'I'm enquiring about the abstract paintings by Edward Abworthy,' she said, 'for the auction. Um…are they all…um still available?'

'Yes, I know the ones you mean,' the girl said brightly. 'But if you're interested in bidding, I have to tell you that unfortunately one of the paintings will not be available,' she said. 'I'm sorry, but the one called Mountain Morning seems to have gone missing. Hello. Hello? Are you there?'

Bay House

1

The house was built on a slope. The front was supported by pylons and there were steps leading down to the beach. You could only access it from the top by navigating the boardwalk which led from the road and over sand dunes which were covered in loose rocks and weeds. There had once been handrails, which were now mostly broken, and some of the boardwalk planks were missing.

Kate Browne knew as soon as she saw the old clapboard building that it was meant to be hers. She walked carefully over the wobbly structure wondering whether the water would cover it at high tide. That didn't matter. In her eyes, it made for the perfect retreat. There was a wide veranda and windows almost all the way around, giving a breathtaking view of the sea and rocky outcrops.

She was accompanied by real estate agent Jack Bainbridge, who had almost given up hope finding a house that his client actually liked. Some of the places he had taken her to she hadn't even bothered to go inside. He was beginning to feel hopeful at last as Kate exclaimed with delight, 'It's perfect, just perfect. Exactly what I'm looking for.'

They had reached the front door and Jack produced an old-fashioned-looking key. He smiled now, mentally working out how much commission this was going to be worth if he could close the sale.

'Well, I guess you want to see inside.' He put the key into the lock. It turned with a little difficulty. 'It's probably a bit rusty,' he remarked, 'but nothing that some oil won't fix.'

Kate looked around eagerly. It wasn't very big – a lounge and dining room, two bedrooms, a bathroom, a reasonably equipped kitchen and a laundry. There wasn't much furniture, just a few chairs, a big old-fashioned bed and a kitchen table.

Kate twirled around, arms out wide with a big grin on her face. 'I'll take it.' She stopped still and looked at Jack, who seemed thunderstruck and a little lost for words.

'But don't you need to think about it?' he asked. Admittedly, he may have been thinking about his commission, but still, he liked to make sure his clients were quite happy about their decision and would not go home and think about it and then change their minds, as sometimes happened.

'I'm sure.' Kate sounded determined. 'Are you sure about the price?' She looked anxiously up at Jack, suddenly aware that, as she was very tall, it was unusual to be looking up at a man instead of down. 'Is there something else you need to tell me? Is there some problem with the house that I won't find out about until afterwards?' She regarded him seriously, as he didn't answer straight away.

He was torn. He wanted desperately to sell this property. It had been on his books for over a year but, at the same time, he was basically a decent chap and he really liked Kate. So he took a breath and decided. 'Well,' he started, 'there maybe is one thing you should know about, not a big deal…'

'I knew it,' Kate sighed. Of course, she thought, there had to be something or else why was it going so cheap. 'OK,' she said, 'what is it? Bad plumbing, flooding? Tell me, Jack, what's wrong with the place?'

'Well, there's supposed to be a ghost.' There: he'd said it. He waited for her to change her mind. Everyone else who had viewed the property had thought it looked spooky and changed their minds after he had mentioned the ghost, so he'd decided not to mention it this time. But he felt bad about that – he preferred to be honest about everything when trying to sell a property. As it happened, he needn't have worried.

'How wonderful! Is that all? A ghost? I don't mind in the least.' Kate regarded him with a relieved smile. 'Ghosts can't hurt you, you know. In fact,' she added, 'they give a house character.' She held out her hand. 'So have we got a deal?'

Jack couldn't believe it. 'Yes, for sure.' he replied as they shook hands. 'I'll get the papers drawn up,' he said, 'and provided there's no problem with the finances, you should be able to move in in, say, a few days. A week at most. Is that OK?'

Kate nodded happily. 'I can guarantee there'll be no problem with the finances.'

Jack handed her a card. 'Well, I'll be in touch. Call me if you need to know anything, or have any questions.'

'Thanks.' Kate put the card into her purse. 'I will.' She thought for a moment. 'There are a couple of things.'

'Anything.' Jack would have done anything for her at this point.

'Well, you did say the power would be on?'

'Yes, I can organise that.'

'And what about the septic? Is that working OK?'

'Yes, that's fine.' He raised his eyebrows questioningly as she hesitated.

'There's one more thing.'

'Anything you need to know, don't be afraid to ask.'

'Could I have the key?' Pleading big blue eyes were gazing at him. .

Jack hesitated for a moment. He wasn't supposed to hand over the key until the closure date. But what the heck. Wordlessly, he pulled the key off the ring and handed it to her.

Then surprisingly, impulsively, she stepped forward and gave him a hug. 'Thanks, Jack.'

It seemed the deal was done.

The next day, Kate started packing. She had been renting a small unit since Granny Rose had died. Six months before, she had inherited everything and discovered that the granny who had lived so frugally had amassed a sizable bank account. There had been no other family, no one to contest the will.

Kate couldn't remember her mother; she had walked away from her marriage when Kate was two years old. She had left her baby daughter with her husband Robert, who then, six months later, managed to drive his car into a tree after leaving the pub in an intoxicated state and killed himself. So Granny Rose, Kate's father's mother, stepped in and she and Kate became part of each other's lives for the next twenty-eight years.

Her mother never came back. Kate tried not to dwell on it too often. She would end up feeling sad. Even after all these years, she could still feel deeply hurt that her mother could abandon her like that. Over the years she had tried to get more information from her grandmother about what really happened. Sometimes she wondered where her mother's family were. She had never known them. It would have been nice, she thought, if they had got in touch. Did they know they had a granddaughter? Did her mother remarry, did she have any half brothers or sisters? What had happened?

It all seemed shrouded in mystery, and Granny was tight-lipped. 'It's all in the past,' she would say, and change the subject when Kate tried to talk about it, but she always had the feeling that her grandmother had been just as hurt as she had, and had tried to shield her from whatever happened, so in the end she didn't pursue it.

But she had to admit she had led a good life. Granny Rose had loved her enough to make up for her lack of parents. Sometimes it was a tough love but she had seen her through school and put up with the tumultuous teenage years. Kate had emerged an attractive, positive, caring human being. Admittedly, she didn't have a boyfriend, which was something Granny Rose used to worry about. 'It's time you thought about settling down,' she would say and Kate would laugh and give her a hug. 'Don't you worry about that, Granny. I'm sure the right one will come along one day.'

The big old house where they both had lived had finally been sold. It had been a happy house, but much too big for Kate on her own. She had mixed emotions, sadness at leaving but excitement for the future, especially since she had discovered the house by the bay, and for the first time in her life she had money to spare in the bank.

Kate had resigned her secretarial job and now was able to spend time doing what she had always wanted to do. Writing. Historical romances, fact mixed with fiction based on the histories of some of the old buildings in the area. Old buildings had a fascination for her, especially the families who had lived in them, the tragedies and scandals, plus the occasional ghost. Kate had always been able to sense whether a house had been a happy home or a sad one and sometimes she would pick up strange vibes. Now she would have time to do some research. As soon as she had seen the house by the beach, she knew there was a history there and she couldn't wait to get started. Plus, the fact that there was supposed to be a ghost as well made it all the more exciting.

A week later, the finances were sorted out with the bank and there was enough money after the purchase for Kate not to worry immediately about getting another job.

She had gone to the real estate office to sign the papers and after it was all done, Jack had asked her if she would like to go for a drink to celebrate. He didn't normally do this with customers but, well, he was, to put it mildly, badly smitten with Kate.

Jack enjoyed his job. He especially enjoyed trying to find a home to suit the client. He knew intuitively what would be right for the person, or family, and generally speaking managed to close the sale. Jack could talk enthusiastically to clients in general about the house he was trying to sell, but when it came to women in a social situation he became tongue-tied, awkward.

Kate, well, she was different. For one thing, she was tall and he didn't have to bend down to speak to her. He could chat to her without feeling he had to prove himself. He liked to read and he liked to have an intelligent conversation with someone now and again. Plus Kate, well, she was, in his opinion, totally gorgeous to boot. So when she happily agreed to go to the pub with him, he couldn't believe it.

They chatted for a couple of hours before she said she had better be going. Truth was, Kate had already started moving things into the house well before it was all finalised, and she couldn't wait to get home.

'Can I call you? Just to see how you're going,' Jack had asked.

'Of course, sure. You must come and visit when I'm settled,' she replied. Maybe I'll have a house-warming and I'll have a few friends over as well.' She held out her hand. 'Thanks, Jack, for all your help and finding my new home.'

He held onto her hand a little longer than need be, perhaps hoping for another hug, but she quickly left.

It had taken a couple of days to move all her things in and get everything settled to her satisfaction. The removalist people were careful carrying all her furniture and the rest of the bits and pieces over the walkway and she gave them a nice tip for their thoughtfulness.

When Kate had been cleaning out Granny's old house, she had to get rid of a lot of things, clothes, lots of knick-knacks, paraphernalia of all sorts. She had had to be ruthless. Old photo albums she kept, though, and when she discovered an old shoebox at the back of Granny's wardrobe containing more photos and letters, Kate had put that aside to check out later. She hadn't got around to it until now.

Kate had set up the spare bedroom as an office, with her computer, a filing cabinet and her old desk and chair which she had brought with her. She had thought about getting the landline connected but decided that her mobile phone would be sufficient for her needs for now. She already had a list of old houses, photographs and histories to help get started, but had already decided there was no place better to start than her new home. She wondered about the origins of the so-called ghost. She had not seen nor heard any signs of a ghost so far, so had decided the first place to begin her research would be the local library, which might have information about her house. She had decided to go the next morning.

In the meanwhile, today she was going to spend some time checking out Granny's shoebox. She went into her office and regarded it sitting on top of the filing cabinet. Kate felt an unexplained trepidation, somehow feeling wary of what she might discover, but her natural curiosity won and she carefully lifted it down and carried it to the kitchen table. It was time to open Granny's shoebox.

2

Carefully, Kate untied the string and lifted the lid, placing it on the table. Inside there was a bundle of letters with a rubber band around them and photographs loosely piled in no apparent order, There was also a large envelope, which Kate put to one side as she started going through the photos.

Most were small old-fashioned sepia-coloured pictures They were all of people taken from various angles and with different backgrounds. Kate peered closely, trying to make out a familiar face. There had been a few taken which she recognised from copies in one of the albums which she had seen before. Her mother, holding her baby daughter about a year old in the garden of Granny's house, and one of her father and mother together, probably taken the same day. He so tall and handsome and her mother Ivy barely as high as his shoulder, her beautiful golden hair blowing in the wind. They looked so happy. There were a few of Granny Rose, and Grandpa, who had died before Kate had been born.

She put these to one side and then went to her desk to get the magnifying glass so that she could see more clearly. She didn't recognise anyone else. Who, she wondered, were all these strangers that were so important that Granny kept all of their pictures? Some had dates on the back, mostly in the forties and fifties, and had names of people she had never heard of.

She looked at the bundle of letters. Hopefully, she was thinking, there might be something there that would give a clue and was starting to open one when the phone rang. Startled, she reached for her mobile, at the same time realising it was a different ring tone. She looked at the old-fashioned landline phone on the kitchen wall. She hadn't had it connected. This was weird. Kate got up from her kitchen chair and went over to the wall. Intrigued, and a bit spooked. She reached for the receiver and put it to her ear. 'Hello,' she said, 'who's there?'

There was a rushing sound and what sounded like a whisper in the wind, a breath, faint words barely discernible.

Kate strained her ears, pulling the receiver as close as she could. 'Hello?' she said again. 'Is somebody there?'

Then she heard it again, just a little clearer but still a whisper. 'Hello, Katy,' it said, and then it went completely quiet.

Eyes wide open with amazement, Kate looked at the phone, pressed the connecting bar a few times. Nothing. She replaced the receiver and shakily sat down again. This was way beyond weird. She tried to think logically. It could have been just a malfunction, wind, something wrong with the phone line. In any case, anyone who needed to get in touch had her mobile number. But Katy? That was the bit that had thrown her. No one called her Katy, except Granny sometimes. Maybe her mother did too. She didn't know, she couldn't remember. Maybe she had imagined it. 'This is doing my head in,' she muttered to herself as mixed confusing thoughts went through her mind.

Then, giving herself a mental shake and trying to forget the strange phone call for the moment, Kate picked up the letter she had started to open. It was postmarked 12.12.87 and addressed to Mrs R. Browne at Granny's address. She started to read.

Dear Mum-in-law,
    I am sorry to leave without saying goodbye After Robert lifted his hand to me I couldn't stay. His drinking has got the better of him. I know he won't hurt Katy, as he loves that baby. I hope you will able to keep an eye on her until I have got settled and then I will come and get her. I will write to you again when I have an address.
    Yours truly, Ivy

Kate put the letter down. Her mother hadn't abandoned her; she was coming to get her. So what had happened? Tears welling, hands trembling a little, she opened the next letter. This was postmarked 11.1.88, one month after the first one.

Dear Mum-in-law,

I am sorry I have not been to collect Katy yet but I am hoping to be settled somewhere soon. I have a friend who is helping me. Please write to PO Box Jindinalup WA and I will get my mail there.

Yours truly, Ivy

Kate put the letter down with a frown. Jindinalup? Where on earth was Jindinalup? She shook her head in frustration and tried the next letter.

17.6.88

Dear Mum-in-law,

I received your letter and am so happy to know that Katy is well and that now she is living with you. I am sorry to hear about Robert and hope he didn't suffer too much. I always thought that the drink would be the end of him. I didn't pick up your letter until after the funeral was over, but I would not have been able to go even if I had wanted to, which I didn't. I am living with my friend Joe, who is a lovely kind man and is looking after me. He says that a small child would be hard to look after as we will be on the move soon, so I hope you don't mind if Katy stays with you for a bit longer. Please give her this teddy bear and tell her I'm always thinking about her.

Yours truly, Ivy

Kate glanced across to the sofa where Mr Bear was sitting. Her teddy had been with her ever since she could remember. His fur was worn away in places and one wobbly eye needed refixing but he had survived twenty-eight years of being crammed into suitcases and cuddled, lost and found again many times. Kate would never part with him. It was her only connection to her mother.

The next letter had been sent by Granny to the same post box in

October 1988 and was marked 'Return to sender'. Frowning now, Kate reached for the remaining envelope, which was addressed to Granny. This one was opened and contained two photographs. No letter, just the snapshots..

Then, picking up the magnifying glass again and peering closely at one of the photos, Kate suddenly gave a gasp and sat back with surprise. Hand trembling a little, she tried to hold it steady as she looked again. There was no mistake: it was her mother, not with her father but with another man. Not so tall as her father, balding, with a big smile and his arm around Ivy's shoulders. She was looking up at him. Kate turned the picture over. There was writing on the back. 'Me and Joe December 1988,' it said. Quickly she made the calculation. She would have been three years old, and it would have been a year after her mother had left.

Kate quickly looked at the other photo. She felt chilled, shaky and shocked to her core as she recognised it. There was still some faded colour left, but it was unmistakably a picture of this house, her house. Taken from the front, the handrails alongside the boardwalk were intact, and there were plants growing either side. It looked pretty and cared for. Kate's mother Ivy was standing there, her hand resting on the railing. She looked relaxed and happy with a long skirt blowing in a breeze. And then, peering closely through her magnifying glass, Kate discovered one more thing. That bump under her mother's skirt. She was pregnant! Turning the photo over, she read, 'At Bay House, January 1989.'

Kate sat transfixed. She felt cold. Then she took a deep breath, got up and put the kettle on. She needed a coffee. She could have done with something stronger but she hadn't found a local wine shop yet, so coffee would have to do.

Then she sat for a while, thinking. There were no more letters. Her mother and this Joe person were actually here in this house in January 1989. It was all so unbelievable. She looked through the letters again to make sure she had missed nothing, then reached for the big envelope which she had earlier put aside. It felt bulky. Perhaps there would be a clue. It had her name on the front in big capitals. 'KATHRYN BROWNE,' it said.

Granny must have been pretty sure I would find it, she thought.

3

Kate still had not opened it when the phone rang again, and she realised the meaning of jumping out of your skin as she sprang up knocking her chair backwards. She stumbled for a moment and was about to go for the wall phone when she realised that it was the familiar ring of 'Ode to Joy' on her mobile.

She grabbed it up. 'Who's that?' her voice was loud, strained. There was a small silence and then she recognised Jack's voice.

'Is that you, Kate? Are you OK?'

The concern in his voice was almost her undoing and her voice wavered a bit, 'Oh, Jack, hello,' she said, trying to sound normal. 'Yes, thanks, I'm OK.' She paused, then blurted out, 'No, actually I'm not OK.'

He didn't waste any time asking what the problem was; he went straight for it. 'Would you like me to come over?' he asked. Then worried, wondering if he had been too forward. Maybe she wouldn't like him to intrude on whatever it was that made her sound so uptight. He waited.

Then, 'Yes please,' she said.

That was enough for him. 'I'll be there in half an hour,' he said. Then smiled as a small voice said, 'OK, see you then.'

Kate put the phone down and regarded the big brown envelope. She felt strangely relieved as she decided to wait until Jack got there before opening it.

Her thoughts went to Harold. He was one of the accountants at the insurance office where she had worked since leaving school. She and Harold had been in a casual relationship for about five years. One of the reasons she had decided to move so far away from her home in Adelaide to here on the peninsula, was for a fresh start away from Harold. She could guess what he would have said if she had told him about the strange phone call and the coincidence of her living in the same house as her mother had all those years ago: 'You're making a big deal out of nothing.' He would scoff at her concerns. He was the most completely insensitive person she had ever known. Plus he was jealous of everything she did that did not directly concern him. She wondered why they had stayed together so long. But she knew why: he had a very strong personality, a take-charge person who always knew what was best for her, and because she liked her job and didn't want to make things awkward, she had just gone along with it.

Harold had a very upmarket apartment in the city, and she had sometimes stayed there. He had all the latest electronic gadgets, and liked to give parties to all his upmarket friends. Kate had enjoyed this for a while, now and again, but was always happy to go back home to Granny's sprawling old house, in its quiet leafy suburb north of the city.

He had belittled her desire to write. 'What on earth would you find to write about?' he scoffed at her one day. 'You're a secretary, not a writer. You're good at writing letters, I'll give you that.' He had smiled condescendingly. 'But that's completely different from writing a book.'

When Kate had given notice at the office, Harold couldn't believe it. 'How could you be so stupid?' he'd shouted at her as she was cleaning out her desk. 'You've got a perfectly good job here. Yyou could even be secretary to the CEO one day. And what about us?'

Then she had completely burnt her bridges, so to speak, as she had burst out with 'I'm sorry, Harold, but there is no us. Not any more.'

He had gazed at her dumbfounded and still had his mouth open when she left.

While waiting for Jack to arrive, Kate tidied up a bit around the house and looked at her watch. It was almost noon, so she had a look in the fridge. She had recently shopped, so there was plenty of salad and the makings for a meal in case she decided to invite him to lunch.

When she answered the knock on the door and saw him standing there with a bottle under one arm, she wanted to give him a big hug but instead just said, 'Hi, Jack, thanks for coming.' She stepped back. 'Come in.'

'Thanks, Kate.' He looked around. 'Wow, you have really got it looking nice.' Then he looked closely at her and lifted up the bottle. 'Would you like me to open this?'

Kate smiled her thanks and nodded. She went to the cupboard and took down two wine glasses, while he opened the bottle, seated himself at the kitchen table and then poured.

He lifted his glass. 'Cheers,' he said.

'Cheers,' Kate responded, and then there was a brief silence as Jack waited for her to start talking.

He was happy to just sit and look at her and sensed that she would start when she was ready.

She indicated the glass of wine. 'I really appreciate this, Jack. Thanks, and thanks for coming.'

Then she started talking. Once she started, she couldn't stop. About the strange phone call, the photographs, the letters, the coincidence of such a thing happening. He waited, not interrupting, saying nothing until she stopped. Then she indicated the big brown envelope, 'So I haven't opened that yet. I waited for you to come.' She looked down at the table. 'I suppose you think I'm quite stupid making a big deal about this.'

He reached over and placed his hand over hers. 'I don't think any such thing. Sure, it's a bit of a puzzle, and I can see why anyone would be a bit freaked out. Tell you what,' he added, 'what say you open that envelope to see if there're any more clues or whatever and then we'll have a think about what to do next.'

'OK.' Kate liked the reassuring sound of 'we' and smiled as she picked up the envelope. She carefully pulled the top open where the old glue was coming unstuck, then tipped it all upside down onto the table, and they both leaned forward to look.

Kate picked up a small box and opened it up. 'Oh, wow!' she breathed. 'Look, Jack, a beautiful ring. It looks like a sapphire and diamonds. It must have been Granny's.' She looked puzzled. 'She had a box of old brooches and some beads, lots of beads, nothing worth anything much. I've never seen this before, though. But then,' she added, 'I never saw her wear any jewellery except her wedding ring.' She slipped it on her third finger. 'Fits perfectly. Wow,' she said again.

Kate picked up one of the folded documents. 'Let's see what this is.' She was feeling a bit excited now. 'Well, this is my birth certificate. I've already got a copy of that. This must be the original. Born 1.12.85. Kathryn Ivy Browne,' she read. 'Mother Ivy Jean Browne, Father Robert John Browne.'

Jack smiled at her, 'Kate, it's your birthday tomorrow.'

She looked confused for a moment. 'So it is. I can't believe I'd forgotten.'

'The big three-O,' Jack grinned. 'I had my thirtieth two months ago.

She put the birth certificate aside and picked up another form.

'Mum's marriage licence, dated 10.9.85.' Kate stopped and looked again at the date. 'Oh, oh.' She handed it to Jack. 'Look. She was six months pregnant with me when they married.' She shook her head. 'How come I never knew that?'

Next was a copy of her mother Ivy's birth certificate dated 20.4.67. 'Mother Jean Ivy McDonald, Father John McDonald', and an address in Dundee, Scotland.

Kate gasped as she handed it to Jack. 'Look, she was born in 1967. That means she was only eighteen when I was born. And look, her family came from Scotland.'

Jack nodded. 'It seems like there's quite a bit to find out.' He took up another document, glancing at Kate, who was looking angry now as well as puzzled. 'You OK?' he asked.

'I should have known all about this. How come Granny never told me anything about this?' She looked at the last document he was holding. 'Well, what's next? Any more surprises?'

He opened it up. 'Well, this one's your dad's death certificate – 6 June 1988. It seems he died of multiple injuries sustained from a car accident.'

'Well, that's no surprise. At least Granny told me about that.' Kate put everything back in the envelope and looked at the last thing from the shoebox, which had been underneath the letters. 'It looks like a roll of film.' She opened the container. 'One of those you have to look at through a projector.'

She handed it to Jack, who unrolled it a bit and held it up to the light. 'Yes, I reckon you're right.' He put it back. 'Tell you what,' he added, 'I'm pretty sure my dad has an old projector. I haven't seen it for years, but I bet it's still somewhere around the place. He never throws anything out.'

Kate was looking excited. 'Do you think you could lend it to me so that I could see what's on this film?'

'Of course. No worries.' Jack replaced the film in the container.

'In the meanwhile,' Kate was putting everything back into the box, 'what do you say we have some lunch?'

'Good idea. Thanks.' He got up from the table. 'What can I do to help?'

'Nothing, I've got some salad and cold meat and it won't take long.' Kate had already started pulling plates out of the cupboard and indicated the cutlery drawer. 'Knives and forks are in there.' She suddenly realised that she was treating Jack like family instead of a guest and anxiously glanced at him, but he was making himself at home in her kitchen as though he belonged there.

Over lunch, she discovered that he worked for his father, who owned the real estate business, and that he had a brother and sister who lived in Sydney. That he had never been married or had a serious long-term relationship. She told him about Harold and about her job. How she missed her friends and hoped to invite some over as soon as she had a few things settled.

Then Jack helped with the washing up and departed. He intended looking for the projector as soon as he could and hopefully bring it back the following day. 'I'll let you know,' he said.

It was only an hour so later that he phoned. 'I've found it,' he said, and Dad has shown me how to work it. So, if you like, I'll come by after work tomorrow. I'll probably be finished around four.'

Jack turned up the following afternoon carrying a big box, and Kate watched anxiously as he took a while to work out what to do, feeding the film onto the reel, and then she took a picture down from the white-painted living room wall to make a space for the projected pictures.

Finally they got it started.

'Oh, wow, it's Mum and Dad's wedding.' Kate was rapt.

Indeed, someone had made a movie at Ivy and Robert's wedding with a very wobbly hand, and the film wavered about between different people. It was in colour but no sound. It seemed to be mostly of people dancing. It was easy to spot the bride and groom, who looked very happy. There was a younger-looking Granny Rose dancing with someone Kate didn't recognise.

Suddenly Kate peered more closely. 'Can you stop it for a minute?' She sounded excited.

Jack nodded, and the whirring sound ceased, as she rushed into the kitchen to pick up the shoe box and brought it back.

She rifled through the photographs. She had remembered seeing the name McDonald on the back of one. 'Yes,' she exclaimed, 'here it is. Look, Jack.' She showed him the picture, then she pointed to two people in the movie. 'See, these two people are John and Jean McDonald. I bet that's Ivy's parents.' Kate stopped then, realisation striking her. 'My other grandparents. So why didn't Granny mention them? She must have known them – they were at the wedding after all. I wonder where they are now. Didn't they know about me? They must have, mustn't they?'

She was so full of questions with no answers. Jack pressed play and they watched more of the film, then she asked him to pause it again.

'I don't believe it,' she said now.

'What is it?' Jack looked intrigued, even though he was concerned for Kate, who was looking agitated again.

'Him. See him?' she pointed to another person facing the camera. 'I recognise him as well.' She brought out the picture of her mother and Joe which had been sent to her granny. 'That's that Joe person.'

She handed the picture to Jack and he studied it closely, then handed it back. 'Yes, you're right.' He looked at her. 'Which means…'

'…that she already knew him, Kate finished. 'She already knew him. When she sent that picture to Granny of them both together and said that a friend was helping her, it was him.'

Kate didn't say any more until the movie stopped. She hadn't recognised anyone else and she sat for a few moments without saying anything.

'Are you OK?' Jack asked her.

Kate nodded. 'I've just got a lot to think about,' she said.

'Yes, I can see that.' Jack hesitated. 'Kate?'

'Yes?'

'As it's your birthday tomorrow, I was thinking, would you like to have dinner with me? Of course,' he hurried on, 'if you've got anything else on, that's fine. I just thought, well…'

'Thanks, Jack,' she smiled. 'Yes, I would like that.'

'That's great.' Jack looked at his watch. 'I have to go. I have an appointment with a client at three o'clock. I'll pick you up around six tomorrow. And try not to worry too much,' he added.

As he left, Kate stepped up and gave him a hug. It seemed the natural thing to do, as was evident by the big grin he had on his face as he waved goodbye.

4

After Jack had left, Kate sat down at her computer again, started a new page and began making notes about what had happened so far. She reminded herself that whatever had happened to her mother and all the other mysteries in the past, including the existence or not of a ghost, she would have to be objective and treat it all like she would if doing regular research for a story. Getting really into it now, Kate started writing down everything she would need to check out. There were so many questions unanswered, but she was cool with it all now. She just had to pretend it was about someone else and not her.

She slept well that night, looking forward to her date with Jack. She had completed a list of things for him to help her check out. The tide was in and she was lulled by the gentle sound of the surf. She was used to the occasional creak and little noises in the house and paid no attention. She felt safe and secure.

When she arose next morning, Kate was surprised to find Mr Bear sitting in the middle of the lounge room carpet. She frowned and picked him up, gave him a cuddle and replaced him on the sofa where he normally sat. She felt just a twinge of excitement and looked around to see if anything else had been moved. Everything seemed to be in place until she noticed one difference. The photograph of Ivy was on top of the closed-up laptop. Kate couldn't remember whether she had left it there or not. She didn't think she had, but there had been so much on her mind yesterday, she supposed she could have.

She had another look at the picture and wondered if it could be enlarged a bit. So she scanned it through the printer, transferred it to the computer and tried enhancing it. The photo was of poor quality and wouldn't go much bigger before going blurry, but she managed about twenty per cent improvement and printed it out. She looked closely and then had a quick intake of breath as she reached for the magnifying glass, concentrating on Ivy's hand resting on the railing. She was wearing a ring which she hadn't noticed before. Kate compared it to the ring she had found in Granny's box. She couldn't be positive but it certainly looked like the same one. Maybe Joe had sent it to Granny after Ivy had died and she had kept it all these years. Who knows, she thought. Just another mystery to add to the others.

Kate went through the still unpacked boxes sitting in the corner of her spare-room-cum-office and found an old frame containing a schooldays picture of herself, took it out and replaced it with the one of Ivy standing in front of Bay House. It fitted nicely. Then she put it on her desk. It was, after all, the last picture she had of her mother.

Later that afternoon, Kate was rummaging through her wardrobe. These days she just about lived in jeans, or shorts and tops. She hadn't been on a date since Harold, and he had always expected her to look well turned out and 'do him credit', as he liked to put it. She didn't think – in fact, she knew – that Jack would not be so critical. But still, she wanted to look passable.

She decided on a simple blue sleeveless number the same colour as her eyes and found her white bag and shoes.

That evening when she opened the door to Jack's knock and saw his smiling look of approval, she knew she had chosen well.

He was holding a bunch of flowers. 'Happy birthday,' he smiled, then kissed her lightly on the cheek.

'Oh,' Kate felt herself blushing. 'Thanks, they're lovely, um…' She flustered a bit. 'I'll just put them in water.'

'Do you like Chinese?' he asked after they were both seated in the car.

'Yes, I love it, but where on earth is there a Chinese restaurant in these parts?'

'Not here in Sandy Bay but further up the coast there is,' he replied.

So after a twenty-minute drive they arrived at Jimmy Chan's Chinese Eatery.

Kate noticed Jack had already booked the table and looked at him in surprise. 'How did you know?' she asked.

'Just guessed,' he grinned.

Kate found herself enjoying the food, the conversation and the evening in general so much that she almost forgot her list of unanswered questions, so while they were waiting for the second course, she pulled out her notepad and a pen from her bag.

Jack looked at her. 'I can guess what you want to talk about,' he smiled, 'but before you start, I'll tell you what I found out today.'

'OK.' Kate put the book down and leaned back. 'So what did you find out?'

'Well, for starters, I found out that the records go back to 1980 and that Bay House was one of the original homes built here. It was a holiday home for some rich people from the city and they used to come every summer.'

'That was first on my list.' Kate burst in. 'That's fantastic. So what else did you find out?'

'Well,' he continued, 'my dad only took over the business five years ago and although he inherited all the old records, they were in a pretty bad state inasmuch as not many details about the tenants were recorded. Just dates. You see, they were all rentals lasting two or three weeks. The owner apparently rented it out when he wasn't living there himself.'

'Well, what about the ghost? Are there any records about the ghost?' Kate wanted to know.

'I couldn't find any mention of a ghost until 1990. And it seems to have been only families with children who reported instances of toys being moved around from one room to another. In one case, doors were heard opening and closing during the night, and in another a whole box of toys had been upturned and were spread all over the floor.'

'Wow.' Kate had been listening, rapt. 'So, anything else?'

'Well, it seemed that generally it was thought to be the spirit of a child roaming around the place but it was enough to freak people out.'

Jack turned as the waiter had appeared with their main course and conversation stopped as they admired the food and then tucked in.

'This is yummy.' Kate was busily trying to manoeuvre chopsticks. 'So carry on, Jack. What else did you find out?'

'Just that the original owner passed away just over a year ago and his inheritors put it up for sale and, as it was slow to sell, the price was dropped dramatically, which is why you got lucky.'

Kate was quiet for a minute. 'So then, the ghost stories didn't start until after Ivy and Joe moved in.'

Jack looked up. 'So?'

'So, well, that's strange, that's all.' Kate wasn't sure what she was thinking. 'Do you think you could find out whether there has been someone renting one of the other shacks for the past twenty-five years or so who might remember Ivy and Joe?'

'Well, sure' I'll give it a go.' Jack was relishing his food. ' What else do you have on your list?'

'Yes, well, I was thinking.' Kate was looking at her notebook. 'If Ivy was pregnant, which I'm pretty sure she was when that picture was taken, then she would have had to go to hospital, wouldn't she? So would you know where the nearest hospital would have been back in 1989?'

'Good thinking. It was probably Jackson Harbour, but I'll check it out and let you know. Anything else?'

'Well,' she glanced at her notes, 'there's the question of whether Joe and Ivy married, and if she had a child, then he or she would be my half sister or brother. Then I have to find out if the McDonalds are still alive, and if they are then why didn't they keep in touch with Granny.' Kate paused. 'If she knew, why didn't she tell me?'

Kate looked so dejected then that Jack reached across the table and took her hand. 'I think that your granny didn't want to upset you when you were too young to understand, and when you got older she put it all in the past. I think she must have loved you very much, Kate, and only wanted the best for you.'

Kate sighed. 'You're probably right. She was always there for me, she was my rock.'

'Tell me, Kate,' Jack asked then, 'why did you decide to come to the peninsula when you decided to look for a house? Did you already know someone here?'

Kate pondered for a moment. 'Well, I never really thought about this before, but I think it was Granny. When I visited her in hospital, I guess she knew she wouldn't be coming home and she told me that I should think about starting afresh, away to somewhere else after she was gone. I told her that I wouldn't be going anywhere, but she persisted and…' Kate stopped and her eyes widened as she remembered. 'She said I should go to the west peninsula, and when I asked her why, she said that it was beautiful country and that I would find what I was looking for.' Kate looked at Jack, eyes wide. 'I've only just remembered that. At the time, I thought she was rambling a bit, being so sick, but I remembered afterwards and I was curious, which is why I drove over here to have a look around. That's when I saw your sign outside the office. It was a spur of the moment thing. I didn't think for a moment that I would actually buy a house here.'

Jack smiled. 'And then you saw Bay House.'

'Yes, and as soon as I saw it I knew that it was exactly what I was looking for. Apart from the fact that this is a beautiful part of the country.' Kate shook her head in wonder. 'Hard to believe, isn't it?'

Jack had no words, he just nodded, and they finished their meal quietly, Kate pondering on the possibility of having a half brother or sister that she'd never met, and Jack thanking fate, or who or whatever was responsible for bringing Kate into his world.

'I think Granny knew.' Kate broke the silence. 'She knew what happened and I'm going to find out. Tomorrow I'm taking a drive to Jackson Harbour hospital and if that doesn't work out, I'll try another one.' She remembered she was going to check out the nearest library, but decided to put that on hold for the time being.

Jack drove Kate home afterwards and walked her to her door. He planted another kiss on her cheek. 'I'll call you.'

She nodded. 'Thanks, Jack, for tonight and everything. I'll let you know how I go.'

'Good, and I'll be checking our records to see if any of your neighbours are long-time tenants, or owners.'

Kate had a big smile on her face as she waved him goodbye. She let herself into her house and then stood stock still as she came to her living room. Mr Bear wasn't in his usual place. She soon discovered him, though. This time he was sitting in the middle of her bed.

Kate was feeling not a little spooked. Then she remembered her words to Jack when he was showing her the house. 'Ghosts can never hurt you.' She had been flippant, and realised it was because she had never actually encountered one, and it was easy to scoff. But this? This was actually happening and now she was intrigued. Her house had happy vibes. She felt at peace here. So why was this happening?

Kate crossed her arms and stood in the middle of the room. 'What are you playing at, Mr Ghost?' she called out. 'Are you trying to tell me something? If you are, then I'll need another clue.'

Then she went to bed. She left Mr Bear where he was, just shifting him over a bit to make room. Tomorrow was another day.

5

When Kate woke the next morning, the first thing she did was check out the bed to see if Mr Bear was still there. He was; he hadn't moved. She carried him through to the lounge room and sat him back on to the sofa. 'You stay there and behave yourself,' she said, aware she was strangely giving orders to a stuffed bear.

She did a quick search around the house to see if anything else had been moved during the night, but everything seemed to be in its place. Then she remembered the ring. She suddenly had a bad feeling and rushed back to the bedroom. She had worn it last night for dinner and put it on the bedside table along with her watch. It wasn't there. The watch was but not the ring. She searched around for a moment in case she had knocked it off during the night but it was nowhere to be seen. 'Oh, no.' She panicked for a moment. This surely can't be happening, she thought.

Quickly she whirled around the house, stopping short when she flung open the door to her office. There it was, sitting on her desk alongside Ivy's photograph. She gave a big sigh of relief, picked it up and put it back on her finger. 'That's going to stay there from now on,' she muttered, and went to the kitchen to prepare breakfast.

Later that day, Kate embarked on her trip to the hospital. It took almost an hour and then another ten minutes to find a car park. When she asked if she could get some information from records twenty-five years ago she was met with a blank stare from the young lady on the information desk.

'I'll try and find out for you,' she said. 'What's your name?'

Kate told her and then was pointed to a seat.

'Wait over there,' the young lady said, and then spoke to someone on the phone.

It was another ten minutes before a harassed-looking nurse appeared. 'Are you Miss Browne?' she asked Kate, who nodded. 'Come with me,' the nurse beckoned. 'I understand you wish to see some old records?'

Kate nodded again and quickly followed the nurse through the hospital and down a level, through some passages to a storeroom with shelves filled with files stacked all around the walls. At the back of the room was an elderly bearded gentleman seated at a desk, peering into a computer. He looked up in surprise as they entered and Kate had the feeling he didn't get many visitors.

'Hello,' he said and stood up. 'Nurse Jones, isn't it?' He smiled, then looked at Kate, who warmed to him immediately. 'And who is this?'

'This is Miss Browne. She would like to see some of our old records.' She regarded Kate curiously. 'I understand you're working on a history project in connection with your family?'

Kate nodded, wondering just what the girl on the desk had actually told the nurse, who continued, 'And this is Jim Carter. He's currently working on our old records. I'm sure he'll be able to help you, so I'll leave you to it.' Then she was gone.

Jim indicated a chair. 'Take a seat, Miss Browne.'

'It's Kate,' she told him. 'Please, call me Kate.' She sat down, bringing the chair closer to the desk and dived into her handbag for her notebook and pen.

'So what can I do for you, Kate?' Jim gave her one hundred per cent of his attention and waited for her to speak.

'Well…' She hesitated for a moment, wondering how to start, then found herself telling him the whole story, apart from the ghost part, which she didn't think was relevant, and finished up with '…and so I thought that maybe she'd come here to have the baby, and to see if there are any records of where she went and whether it was a boy or a girl, and whether there's any record of the father.' She stopped for breath and looked anxiously at Jim, who had been listening with great interest.

'Well,' he started, 'first of all, back then, nothing was computerised. It was all in these files.' He indicated the computer. 'I'm transferring some of the old ones onto the computer. It's quite a job and it'll take a long time, but I don't mind. They leave me alone. It's this or retirement, and it gives me something to do. So let's see,' he added, 'what date are we looking for precisely?' He raised his eyebrows with his question, and looked kindly at her. He could see that this was really important for Kate.

'Well, see, that's the problem. I have a photo where it looks as though she's pregnant, taken in January 1989, so it would have been sometime after that. So say between January and April 1989.'

Jim was on his feet heading towards a bank of files across the room. 'And her full name?' he asked.

'Well,' Kate hesitated, 'that's another thing. Her name was Ivy Jean Browne, but she may have married again, so it could have been something different.' Kate sounded forlorn, thinking that it was going to take a while going through all the old records. 'I'm sorry to be such a nuisance,' she apologised. 'The thing is, my mother might not even have come here. This is the first hospital I've tried.'

But Jim was coming back, smiling and holding a bulging box file. 'This was the only hospital in these parts back in those days. It was much smaller then – it's been added onto over the years.' He indicated the file. 'Now let's see what we can find.' He regarded Kate over his glasses,. 'And believe me, young lady, you're not a nuisance, you've brightened up my day.'

He sat down and opened the box. There was a pile of smaller manila files inside.

Kate held her breath as he rifled through.

'This is from Maternity 1989. If it's anywhere, it'll be in here.' He stopped and took out a file. 'This could be it. March 1989. Mother Ivy Jean Richardson, father Joseph Richardson.' He looked up at Kate, who was leaning over the table trying to read upside down. 'Could this be it? It's not Browne, but I don't think there would have been any other Ivy Jeans here at the same time.' He continued to read the notes, then stopped. His face saddened as he passed over the file. 'Perhaps you'd better read it for yourself,' he said quietly, and just watched as Kate read it through, and then again for a second time, her eyes welling with tears as she finally put it down.

Jim got up and came around the desk gently patting her shoulder. 'Would you like a cup of tea or coffee, Kate?'

She nodded silently. 'Thanks, I think I would. Tea please, milk and one sugar.'

He left and she picked up the file again, carefully going through all the information. By the time Jim came back with two cups of tea and a plate of biscuits, she was still shaken but now regaining some composure.

'Thanks, Jim. This must be her. She was with someone called Joe, which of course would have been Joseph. They must have married. You know,' she continued, 'in my heart I think I knew. She would have got in touch if she had still been alive.' She handed the file back to him. 'It says there that the baby girl was named Bethany Rose, she was one month premature and that Ivy died of a haemorrhage and heart failure. But the baby survived.' Kate's face brightened. 'The baby survived.' She sipped her tea, deep in thought. 'So do you think I could get a copy of all this information, Jim? Then I can take it home and read it all properly. The next thing I have to do is to try and find out what happened to Bethany.' She smiled. 'I have a sister – well, a half sister, I suppose – but still that's good news, isn't it?'

Kate sadly took her leave of her new friend Jim, with copies of all the information and a little comforted by the knowledge that somewhere Bethany was hopefully alive, and wondering whether she knew that she had a big sister called Kate who was going to track her down.

6

When Kate arrived home, she phoned Jack. 'She's dead,' she blurted out as soon as he answered. She had been going to wait and tell him when she felt calmer; she had thought she was, and had got it all together, but as soon as she heard his voice she couldn't stop herself, and felt tears welling again.

'Kate, I'm so sorry.' He sounded concerned, caring. 'Would you like me to come over?'

'No, it's OK, thanks, Jack. I'll be OK.' She gathered herself. 'It's just that I went to the hospital today and found out what happened. I just wanted to let you know. I'll tell you all about it later.' She stopped and thought. 'Would you like to come over for tea tomorrow evening?' She managed a laugh. 'That's if you're prepared to risk my cooking. I have a lot to think about at the moment,' she added.

'Of course, that'd be great. I've got some information for you too,' he added, 'so we'll talk about it then.' He stopped for a moment. 'Kate?'

'Yes?'

'Um, well, yes, OK, I'll be there about six.'

'OK, bye.'

That evening, Kate sat outside on her deck, slowly sipping the last of the wine. It was quiet, peaceful, and the tide was on its way out, the sea looking gorgeous, reflecting a golden sunset. She felt calm now. More at peace than she had been in a long time. Sad, because the mother she never really remembered was dead, but at least now she knew why she had never heard from her again.

There were still unanswered questions, though. What happened to Bethany and Joe? She wondered what Jack had found out. Then she thought a lot about the ghost, or spirit or whatever it was.

When Kate went to bed that night, she took Mr Bear with her and left her ring on. Next morning, everything was in its place. Nothing had been moved and she smiled to herself. She had an idea that she might have figured something out. It was a bit bizarre, and she couldn't wait to tell Jack and see what he thought.

Kate tidied the house and did some grocery shopping to make a meal that she could cook without messing it up.

Jack arrived on time with another bottle under his arm. Dinner was under way and Kate had been looking forward to the evening.

The roast chook and vegies were being devoured with relish by Jack, who would have happily settled for a sandwich if need be, before he broached the subject, which he thought Kate might have been reluctant to discuss. She hadn't; she just wanted to enjoy dinner first.

'Kate, are you OK to talk about all this stuff now? Do you want to hear what I've found out?'

She nodded, 'Yes, I'm fine. It was a shock, but really I think I knew, or at least guessed.' She drew a breath. 'My mother died in childbirth. She had a baby girl, Bethany. She was married to Joe, Joseph Richardson, and that's about it. There was no other address except this one, so I don't know how long they were here or where Joe went when he left. Or what happened to the baby.' Kate regarded Jack solemnly. 'There, that's it. So what's next?'

Jack put down his fork and sat back. 'Well, I think I've found a couple of people who have been coming here on and off for the past thirty-odd years. Mrs and Mrs Johnson who rent the shack at number 3. That's just down the road. As it happens, they arrived two days ago. I spoke to Bob Johnson on the phone and they'd be happy to talk to you.' Jack smiled at Kate's expression of delight. 'What do you think? We could take a walk along there after tea.' He considered a moment. 'That's if you'd like me to come with you. If you'd rather go on your own, that'd be fine and you could go tomorrow. I can't promise anything, mind. They may not remember anything at all. It's a long time ago. So what do you think?'

Kate didn't have to stop and think. 'Of course I'd like you to come with me. And we'll go this evening.' She jumped up and started clearing the plates away. 'This is brilliant. Thanks so much, Jack.'

He helped her clear up and half an hour later they were walking down the steps to the beach along the sand. They stopped in front of the third house along.

A couple of people were sitting in deckchairs, outside an old-looking shack, and they waved at Jack and Kate as they hesitated below. 'Come on up,' they shouted. 'We thought you might be along.'

Bob and Betty Johnson were typical Aussies. In their fifties, laid-back, friendly, welcoming. They produced beers and two more chairs. There were handshakes, and the conversation flowed as it does among new friends prepared to like one another., Betty being the chatty one and her husband Tom quieter and happy to sit back and listen.

'So, what can we help you with? Mind you, the old memory isn't as great as it used to be, but we'll do our best.' Bob looked at his wife, 'Betty's better at recalling old stuff than me.'

Betty was eager to please and looked enquiringly at Kate.

'Were you here in 1989?' Kate started. 'Twenty-six years ago? I'm trying to get some information about two people who lived in my house at number 1 – Bay House.'

'1989.' Betty pursed her lips and frowned, adding some more wrinkles to her forehead. 'What was their name then?' she asked.

'It was Ivy and Joe Richardson. She was pregnant.' Kate waited while Betty contemplated.

Her brow cleared and she nodded, looking sad. 'Can I ask, why do you want to know?'

'She was my mother,' Kate said simply. 'I've only just found out about her.'

Betty looked astounded for a moment then reached across and grabbed Kate's arm. She turned to Bob. 'Darl, I think this is Bethany.' She looked askance at Kate. 'I thought you said your name was Kate?'

'Yes, I am Kate. So do you remember?'

Betty had closed her eyes and sat very still.

'Betty?' Kate hoped she wasn't dropping off to sleep.

Betty opened her eyes. 'You have the same golden blonde hair as Ivy,' she said then, 'but she was a little thing.' She looked at Kate. 'And you're quite tall, aren't you?'

Kate persisted. 'So you remember? You remember Ivy?'

Betty let go of Kate's arm and looked at Bob. 'Don't you remember, darl? They were such a lovely couple. She was so excited about the baby. They came over for tea a couple of times and you went fishing with Joe.'

Bob was slowly nodding. 'Well, I must say,' he said, 'it's all coming back a bit now you mention it.' He looked at Betty then at Kate. 'She died, didn't she?'

There it was straight out. Betty gave her husband a stare and then turned to Kate. 'I'm sorry, Kate. Yes, she died when she had the baby.'

Kate nodded. 'Yes, I know.'

'You know?'

'Yes, I know,' Kate repeated. 'The thing is, do you know what happened to Joe and the baby? Where they went?'

'You say she was your mother?' Frustratingly, Betty didn't answer her question.

Kate tried again. 'Yes, I was living with my grandmother. I would have been about four years old. So do you know where they went?' she persisted. 'I need to know.'

Betty turned to Bob again. 'Imagine that, darl. Ivy already had a child. Well, I never knew that.' She looked at Kate's anxious face and hastily continued. 'Well, as far as I remember, they went to Queensland, didn't they? Joe had family there. He was that upset. He was in a bad way. She was four weeks premature and the baby had to stay in hospital for another three weeks before they let him take her home. By that time, we had to go back. I remember we left before he did. I think we only had a couple of weeks. It was school holidays and our two were quite a handful.'

She rattled on a bit more about their children and holidays and more tourists and having to book the shack well in advance these days, before asking, 'Did you say it was your house? Did you buy it then?' She stopped for breath and looked closely at Kate. 'You all right, love? Did you want to know anything else?'

Jack had not said a word until now. He looked at Kate, who seemed to be struck dumb, and he asked the question that he knew she needed to ask. 'So do you have an address by any chance?'

'Well, we did keep in touch for a while but I haven't heard in a long time, years. Hang on a tick.' Betty suddenly got up and went inside the house. It was a couple of minutes before she reappeared holding a big photo album. 'I always bring this with us when go away,' she said. 'In case the house burns down. I wouldn't like to lose all the family photos.'

She rifled through the pages and eventually stopped, putting her finger on a picture. 'That's them, Joe and Bethany.' She pulled the picture out from the page. 'Here, you can have it if you like.' She handed the photo to Kate.

It was a picture of Joe and the baby. He was sitting in a chair in what appeared to be a garden, with a big house in the background. He was looking down at the baby. Kate turned the picture over. There was writing on the back. 'Me and Bethany at home in Brisbane August 1989.'

'I always kept photos which reminded me of our holidays, which is why it's in there. Joe must have sent that one after he'd got home. I think there may have been a letter but it's all too long ago now.'

'Brisbane? He lived in Brisbane.' Kate gazed at the picture. 'Oh, thank you, Betty. I appreciate this. I don't suppose you have any address where I could get in touch, do you?'

'Sorry, love, that's it, I'm afraid. That picture's about twenty-five years old, so they could be anywhere by now. Besides, little Bethany would be all grown-up and maybe married and gone who knows where. I often used to wonder how they got on, but really I haven't thought about them for years. Now you turning up out of the blue like this, well, that's really something, isn't it?'

Kate sensed that Betty would have like to know more of the story, but she needed to go home. There was too much to think about. She looked at Jack, 'I think it's time we made a move.'

He nodded and rose, turning to shake hands with Bob. 'Thanks for the beer and the chat. We'll have to catch up again.'

'Yes,' Kate added. 'Thanks so much for everything. It's really appreciated, especially the photo.'

As they made their way back down the steps, Kate stopped and turned. 'By the way, have you heard anything about a ghost in my house?'

Betty and Bob looked at one another enquiringly.

'Load of rubbish,' Bob laughed. 'It was a family with a load of kids, reckoned their toys kept disappearing and reappearing again.'

'Yes,' Betty chimed in, 'and lights kept coming on by themselves. Silly stuff like that. If you want my opinion, it was all their imagination and carelessness.' She stopped and thought. 'But the last family we spoke to when we were here the year before last, I think it was, I do remember they went home early. They were trying to get a refund, but I don't reckon they did. I don't remember now.' Betty sounded doubtful. 'Maybe there was something in it after all.'

Bob was having none of it. 'Absolute nonsense,' he said. 'Don't you worry, Kate, I'm sure there's nothing to worry about. That's a lovely old house you've got there, the best one in the street. Certainly better than this old place. Anyway, call and see us again, won't you?'

So they all waved goodbye.

Kate and Jack walked along the sand back to her home in silence. Tomorrow, Kate thought, it would be time to visit Mr Google.

7

The next morning, Kate booted up the computer and got on to Google. She had been thinking about the best way to find someone.

Joe would probably be in his late forties or early fifties. It was possible that Bethany might have changed her name, so she decided she'd start with Joe.

She typed in 'Joseph Richardson'. No search suggestions found it said. So she tried 'Joe Richardson'. That was more like it. There were twenty-five Joe Richardsons from all over the world. Please don't let him have travelled overseas somewhere, she thought. I'll never find him. She scrolled down until she found three possibles. One was a shoe manufacturer in Sydney, and there were two in Queensland. Kate stopped for a moment. She had no idea what business Joe had been in, and anyway he might not have a website. She wondered if the Johnsons knew. She had exchanged mobile phone numbers with Bob Johnson the night before and, taking a chance, gave him a call. She hoped Betty wouldn't answer. Much as she liked her neighbour, she didn't want to get into a long chatty conversation right now.

Luckily, Bob answered. 'Well, let me think,' he said when she asked him the question. 'I really have no idea. Hang on. I'll see if Betty can remember.' Then he was gone for a few minutes, returning sounding puffed. 'She was out hanging some washing. Anyway, she said to tell you that she thought she remembered Joe being a journalist for the a newspaper, but couldn't say which one, and that he had to travel around a fair bit.' He sounded anxious. 'But you know she could be wrong. Sometimes she can't tell the difference between remembrance and imagination. Haven't you had any luck tracking him down?'

'Well, I'll have better luck now I've got something to start with,' Kate said. 'Thanks a lot for that, Bob. I'll let you know how I go.'

The next job was to find a list of newspapers published in Queensland. There were quite a few, including local community publications, and she started writing addresses and phone numbers down, realising that all this would be a waste of time if he wasn't even in Queensland. But determined now, she started at the top. She had already decided what to say and tried it out on the first one.

'I'm trying to track down a journalist, but I don't know the name of the paper he worked for. Could you please find out if you had a Joseph or a Joe Richardson working for you back in 1989 and whether by any chance he's still employed by you?'

The first few she tried were outright: 'No, sorry, never heard of him.'

Then there was one who suggested she write in with a request and they would check the archives. Another said no, but suggested another newspaper to try, which she did and had no success.

Then she tried the *Sunday Sun* and found a helpful girl who repeated the name – 'Joseph Richardson?'

Kate crossed her fingers as the girl thought for a moment.

'Oh,' she said, 'that would be Joe Richardson. He has a weekly opinion piece. Is that the one you mean?

Kate tried to hide her excitement and sound businesslike. 'Yes, that sounds like him. Could you give me his phone number, please?'

'Oh, I'm sorry,' the girl sounded regretful, 'we're not allowed to give out private numbers. Joe doesn't come into the office very often – he sends his work in by email. But I'll be happy to pass on a message if you leave your number. So he can ring you. Would that be OK?'

'Yes, fine, if you could do that, I'd appreciate it.' Kate gave her phone number. 'Thanks so much.'

'You're welcome, but it could take a while,' the girl added. 'He may be away on an assignment.'

Kate gave her thanks again and said goodbye. She sat back and took a few deep breaths. Then doubt crept in. Could she have found the right Joe so soon? What were the odds? Please let it be him, she thought. Please let him ring back.

Next she rang Jack to update him on her progress but had to leave a message for him to call her. Then she made a coffee and went outside to sit on her deck, where she always felt calmed. She sat back with her eyes closed. Then out of the blue a sudden breeze came up unexpectedly. She felt a soft touch on her face as her hair brushed her cheek, feeling like a gentle stroke from a soft hand. Kate opened her eyes and jerked forward as she sensed an unexplained fleeting presence for a brief moment, then it left as quickly as it came. All was calm again. Kate smiled as she touched her cheek.

It was only a couple of hours before her mobile rang.

'Hello, Kate speaking,' she said and held her breath as a woman's voice answered.

'Oh, hello…um. There was a message on my father's phone to call you. He's away at the moment but if it's important I could get a message to him.'

The voice was friendly, polite, and Kate felt a shock wave course through her body. She could scarcely speak.

'Hello?' The voice again. 'Are you there?'

'Yes.' Kate sounded shaky. Then finally it came out. 'Are you Bethany?'

'Yes, that's me. How did you know my name?'

'I'm Kate Browne. My mother was Ivy. She married Joe, your father. So I guess that makes me your sister.' There: she'd said it. She waited.

Then the voice on the other end returned. She sounded excited. Incredulous. 'Kate? I can't believe it. This is so unreal, you know. My father told me about you.' She stopped for a moment. 'How do I know you're Kate?' she asked, sounding a little wary. This isn't some kind of joke, is it?'

So Kate told her the story, ending up with how she came to buy Bay House, and then they talked. Bethany told her how Joe had rang her grandmother's house and that the phone had been answered by a man who had told him that Kate had moved away and he had no forwarding address.

This was unbelievable. 'When was this?' Kate asked.

'Oh, probably about five years ago now,' said Bethany, and Kate knew it must have been Harold answering the phone on one of the times he had been visiting her and Granny was out. He had never mentioned it. He would have been suspicious of any male caller and he had lied.

'I never knew,' she said now. 'I never got the message.'

Bethany told her that she always called at her father's place when he was away, to water the plants, and that she was buying her own home. That he would be back in a few days and how excited he would be when he heard that Kate had found them.

They chatted like sisters for an hour. Kate was so happy when they eventually said their goodbyes she could scarcely contain herself and rang Jack again, but had to leave another message.

She remembered afterwards that when talking to Bethany, she hadn't mentioned the so-called ghost. But that could wait for when she visited; Bethany had insisted that she go to Queensland some time soon, then she could talk to them both together. She was fairly certain she knew now what had been happening and wanted to share her thoughts with Jack, taking the chance that he would be sceptical but knowing in her heart she was right, unbelievable as it might seem.

The knock on the door came about an hour later. It was Jack. They started talking at the same time and he was saying that she sounded so excited when she left her message he had decided to come over to find out her news, when the phone on the kitchen wall rang.

They both stopped talking at the same time and stood still, looking askance at the phone on the wall, which had still not been connected.

'Aren't you going to answer it?' Kate had frozen. Jack gave her gentle push.

She almost fell towards the phone and grabbed it from its cradle. 'Hello?' she said.

Jack drew close and she held the phone out a bit so he could hear as well. It was like the sound of the sea whispering through a conch shell.

'Goodbye, Katy,' it whispered. 'Goodbye.'

'Goodbye, Mum,' Kate whispered back. 'Goodbye.'

Blood Will Be Spilled

Tommo and Ben had joined the local amateur dramatic society, who were being adventurous and attempting to make a small movie, shooting various scenes in different locations around town. They had been asking for a few volunteers to take part in some crowd scenes, some of which were to be shot at the local pub. The story was about re-enacting history and the story of building workers who had been forced to join unions or lose their jobs. There had been a great deal of unrest at the time, and was all part of the town's history, causing fights to break out and general turmoil resulting in the death of the ring leader, Sam Holden.

It had been Tommo's idea to start with. 'Come on, mate.' He was buying Ben a beer. 'They want twenty people to have a barney in the pub. We could do that. No worries. Plus we get paid.'

'How much?' Ben wanted to know, sounding just a bit interested now that cash was mentioned.

'I dunno, but it'll probably be travel expenses, petrol money or something like that. So what do you say? Shall I put your name down? It'll be a bit of a laugh if nothing else. Besides, the missus is off visiting her mother again. So I've got some free time for a change, and you're between jobs, aren't you? What have you got to lose?'

So in the end Ben agreed, and a couple of days later they both fronted up at the community hall, where they were to be processed and checked out along with all the other local hopefuls who couldn't wait to get their faces on the telly.

'I need a few people with good loud voices.' The director Marty Marks was an American friend of the producer who had offered his services as a favour. He was looking a little frazzled as he sorted out the no-hopers from the possibles. Some people had been sent home and the likely ones had been sent to one side of the room. There were just a dozen blokes left, all between the ages of twenty and forty, Ben and Tommo among them.

Marty was dishing out sheets of paper to everyone. 'I want you to read this carefully,' he said, 'and then when I call you, please step forward and read the line that I tell you to.'

All the blokes looked warily at the paper handed to them. Lines? They didn't expect to have to say anything specific. What was going on? A few of the cocky ones who thought this was going to be a piece of cake weren't looking so sure of themselves.

'OK.' Marty pointed at Tommo. 'You begin. Just read the first line.'

Tommo held the paper out a bit – he couldn't see too well without his reading glasses, but luckily this was a fairly big printout. He drew in his breath. 'This means war,' he said.

'Come on,' Marty shouted. 'Put some guts into it. You're about to have a rebellion. You're angry. Let's hear it again.'

Tommo tried again. He tried to think. Angry, he had to be angry. 'THIS MEANS WAR,' he bellowed.

Marty grinned. 'Well done,' he said. 'Much better.' He turned to Ben. 'OK, you're next. You can read the second line. And give it some power. Remember, you're having a fight. This is all about exploiting workers. You're angry. Go,' he pointed to Ben.

Ben had no problem. 'BLOOD WILL BE SPILLED,' he yelled, and threw his fist into the air for good measure. Then went a little red as all the guys clapped.

'Well done.' Marty was looking a bit more hopeful. Maybe they weren't such a a lot of dead beats after all.

He went through the rest of the blokes as they all read different lines. There were ten parts in all. One by one they were allocated to different people. They were told to remember them; they were to be shouted out during the take. Each person who had a line to say had to remember the one just before his, so that they were shouted out in sequence.

Then they had a practice. There were a few stuff-ups as some people came in too quickly, some forgot their lines and some forgot to come in at all, but in the end they all managed it, to Marty's partial satisfaction. He wasn't happy, not by a long way, but at least they'd made a start.

Tommo ended up with 'WE'RE NOT PUTTING UP WITH THIS,' and Ben was given the line that he first read. 'BLOOD WILL BE SPILLED.'

They were told to go home and practise. They were even given a list of everybody's lines so that they knew whose came directly before theirs. Then they were told to come back in two days when the scene was to be shot in the local pub.

There was much excited muttering as the guys left.

Tommo punched Ben in the arm. 'What d'you reckon then, mate? We're going to be in a movie.' He was sounding quite excited.

Ben shook his head doubtfully. 'I dunno,' he muttered. 'Suppose we stuff it up. We'll look like right idiots.'

'What can we stuff up?' Tommo was scornful. 'All we gotta do is remember a few words. How hard is that?' He patted Ben on the back. 'You worry too much, mate.'

So they went home. 'BLOOD WILL BE SPILLED,' Ben muttered to himself. All that night and the next day he repeated it over. Then worried. Should he put the emphasis on the BLOOD will be spilled, or on the WILL? Blood WILL be spilled. Or perhaps he should stress the word SPILLED. Blood will be SPILLED. In the end he decided he would emphasise every word, then he couldn't go wrong.

The next Wednesday evening, everyone turned up again, this time at the pub where the action was going to be. There were a couple of cameramen, microphones and other paraphernalia and general chaos as Marty tried to get everyone in their places. There were a good few extras for atmosphere, and there were also some of the regular locals and their wives who happened to be in the pub at the time, sitting around the tables looking as normal as could be expected given the exciting circumstances.

Tommo and Ben were sat together with two of the other blokes, one of whom was a local red-haired Scot called Jocko. He was known to be a heavy beer drinker and always up for a fight when he'd had too much. He was already on his third glass. Marty didn't know that of course, or he probably wouldn't have included him. Anyway, they got started.

'Now, in this scene, there's a lot of angry crowd mutterings.' Marty was speaking into the mike. 'I need you to talk among yourselves, as loudly as you like, and when I give the nod to Bob Jackson over there, who's playing the part of Sam Holden, he'll stand up and give his speech. After he's finished, then that's the cue for the person who has the first line to stand up and shout it out.' Marty turned to one of the men. 'That's you, Ned, isn't it?'

Ned nodded.

'Good.' Marty looked over the actors. 'Then one by one you'll stand up and say your lines. One after the other. Not directly after – give a little time. Make it sound spontaneous. OK then, Bob, off you go.'

Bob had done a few amateur dramatics in his time and was one of the few people there who had learned his lines. He gave a convincing speech and then sat down.

Ned immediately stood up and shouted, 'WE DON'T HAVE TO LISTEN TO YOUR RUBBISH. YOU'RE WASTING YOUR TIME.'

Then, after Marty started making frantic winding up motions to get people going, they started getting into it and began talking. The second person took a while to remember to shout out his bit, but then he managed it. Some people forgot altogether, but in the end they managed to get through the scene.

Marty was shaking his head and rolling his eyes. 'OK, everyone, that wasn't too bad.' He sighed. 'Now we'll try it again, and this time, try and concentrate on what you have to say, and the rest of you can call out whatever you like. I need to get more atmosphere. You're an angry mob. You hate unions. You aren't prepared to listen. So let's start over.'

The next time, most of them had got it right. When it came to Ben's turn, he shouted out 'BLOOD WILL BE SPILLED' with such conviction that everyone banged their tables. 'Yeah,' they yelled.

Marty looked a lot happier now and stood up with almost a smile. 'Right, everyone. Now we're going to start shooting. This will be a take. Places, everyone. Right Bob, off you go.'

Bob really got into it then. He made his speech with such forcefulness and passion, everyone looked at him in awe for a moment, then Ned jumped up and shouted out his line.

'Wow.' Ben turned to Tommo. 'That was fantastic,' he whispered.

'Why are you whispering?' Tommo said. 'We're supposed to be talking amongst ourselves.' He had a sip of beer. 'It was pretty decent of them to give us all free beer.' He nudged Ben. 'Watch out,' he said. 'I think you have to say your bit after the next bloke. I don't have to go until nearly the end.'

Marty was looking slightly dismayed. As soon as all his actors had realised the cameras were actually rolling, they had quietened. They were all concentrating on coming in on time. Even the regular patrons had stopped talking and were watching the action. All the charged atmosphere was disappearing. He was losing the momentum he was looking for.

Ben was waiting anxiously. He took a sip of beer, then all too soon realised that the bloke before him had stood up and shouted, 'THIS MEANS WAR,' which meant it was his turn.

Ben still had his beer in his hand as he stood up, waved it over his head and shouted, 'BEER WILL BE SPILLED.'

He realised immediately what he had said and, totally mortified, looked across to Marty, who was shaking his head in disbelief, about to call, 'CUT,' but Ben's hand holding his half finished beer went sideways, tipping it over the head of Jocko, who immediately uttered a curse and stood up, knocking his chair backwards.

'What d'you think you're doing, you stupid bastard.' He threw a punch Ben's way as Tommo intervened.

'It was an accident,' he started to say, but suddenly Jocko's mate got in on the act and knocked Tommo's beer out of his hand. Then the next table got involved and it all started – a free-for-all barney like the pub hadn't seen for a long time. The barman tried to calm things down but was ignored. Tables were overturned, glasses broken and the regular patrons promptly left. Bob, who realised his character didn't get killed until the third act, decided he wasn't taking any chances and disappeared quietly out the side door.

Marty, however, was now grinning from ear to ear. This was more like it. A real brawl like he couldn't have rehearsed if he'd tried a hundred times. He gestured to the cameramen. 'Keep going,' he shouted. 'Make sure you get it all.'

So they did.

Eventually, Marty shouted, 'CUT,' in the microphone. He had to call it three times before anyone took any notice, but by then they had all had enough and it quietened down.

Tommo and Ben surveyed at the mess.

'Mate,' Ben managed to say. He had blood on his knuckles and he looked at Jocko, who was lying on a broken chair and sporting a bloody nose. 'I don't think that was supposed to happen.' He looked across at Marty, who had a strange dazed expression on his face. As though he had just witnessed an out-of-life experience.

'I didn't get to say my line.' Tommo sounded a bit aggrieved. 'After I took the trouble of learning it and everything.'

Marty had taken up the microphone again. 'OK, you can all go now. Great job, everyone.' He turned to the barman. 'Sorry about the mess. We will of course pay for any damages.' He looked around the room then spotted Ben. He beckoned. 'You, Ben, is it? Yes, Ben. Can I have a few words?'

Tommo gave him a push, as Ben didn't look like he was going to move. He was probably going to get a bollocking for saying the wrong line.

Marty held out his hand and Ben hurriedly wiped his on his now beer-stained pants before shaking it.

'Thanks, Ben.' Marty beamed at him. 'It looks as though I have you to thank for saving the day. That was pure genius. It sure got things going, and we got it all on film. So thanks again.' He patted Ben on the arm. 'That was absolutely first class.'

Ben couldn't speak. He just smiled and nodded.

'You must have known that spilled beer would make more of an impact than spilled blood.' Marty shook his head. 'Unbelievable. You Aussies are absolutely unbelievable.' And still shaking his head, he turned and left.

'Well, what did he say?' Tommo wanted to know.

'He said we're unbelievable.' Ben looked bemused. 'He said I saved the day.'

They looked at Jocko, who was heading unsteadily towards the door.

Tommo picked a chair up from the floor, tested the legs and then and sat on it. 'Well, I'll drink to that.' He looked around at the mess. Well, I would if I still had a glass.' He looked at his bloody knuckles. 'On second thoughts, maybe I'll call it a day.' He looked at Ben. 'What d'you reckon, mate?'

'Yeah, let's go.'

Butterfly Stickers

Liz was beginning to realise that catching a train to the city instead of going in her car wasn't something she would be doing again if she could help it. She had thought it would easier than trying to find a park in town. Now on her way home again, it was rush hour and she hadn't been able to find a seat.

Liz clutched her bag tightly to her chest as she tried to find a spot that didn't involve standing too close to anyone else. She had become uncomfortably aware of a man standing near the door, who was staring at her. She wondered at first if it was someone she knew. She had caught his eye while looking around for a seat. He had been staring with such intensity that Liz had quickly looked away, feeling embarrassed and just a little threatened.

She should have been used to people looking at her by now, she thought. It wasn't her fault that she was so tall. She knew she was considered attractive and sighed to herself. She hated being stared at. Sometimes she wished she looked just ordinary and unremarkable, like everyone else.

The train was nearing Liz's stop and she got ready to jump off quickly. She pushed her way through to the door at the rear of the train, got her car key ready, left as soon as the train stopped and hurried out to the car park. Then she drove away as quickly as she could.

That evening, as Liz was about to pull the blind down on the front window, she noticed a car parked across the road in front of her elderly neighbour Nelly's house. A bit strange, she thought. I wonder if she has a visitor. Old Nelly never had visitors, just the district nurse, who called regularly in the mornings, but never in the evenings.

Liz was still pondering this, and wondering if the old lady was OK, when she saw a sudden light in the front of the parked car. Just a quick flash, but enough to realise there was someone sitting there who had just lit a cigarette. Liz quickly drew the blind down, then turned off the light. She went back to the window, peered out again and studied the car. She didn't recognise the make, but the street light just up the road cast a glow, and it was, she decided, definitely blue.

She wondered what she should do. She had a few options. The most obvious was to mind her own business. Or she could quietly go out the back door, through the garden, then along the alley which passed along behind the houses and came out further along back up the road. Then she could sneak up behind the car and get the number. Or perhaps she should ring the police (and tell them what – someone is sitting in a stationary car across the road?). Don't be stupid, she thought.

Maybe, she decided now, it's someone whose car has broken down and they are waiting for the RAA. So perhaps I'll just have a coffee and check again later to see if it's still there.

After dinner, she remembered to check the window, and peeked through the blind. The car had gone. Good, she thought. It was probably nothing to worry about after all.

Liz was employed by the local newspaper to write a weekly column for the social pages. Her trip to town had been to report on a wedding but she had hoped for something more challenging. A couple of days ago she had pleaded with Ollie Jackson, the editor of the *Bulletin*. 'I've been doing the social columns for six months now. When can I start doing some real stories?' she had asked him.

Ollie had looked over his glasses at her and said nothing for a minute. 'I'll tell you when you're ready,' he said. 'You're still a rookie.' He held up a hand as Liz started to speak again. 'That's it, Liz. OK, you're doing fine at the moment, but don't push it.' He thought for a moment again. 'Another three months, then we'll see.'

In the meanwhile, Liz had to curb her impatience, and do the best job she could. Today's wedding reception had had many local identities in attendance and Liz had managed to get an interview with several of the guests. It had been held at lunchtime in the gardens of a lovely manor house north of the city. Jenny the bride had looked beautiful and she had been happy to chat with Liz. The father of the bride, Bob Maynard, was a well known property developer, and an overbearing buffoon in Liz's opinion. She had been shocked when she overheard him telling someone that his daughter deserved the best and 'that wimping idiot' was not it.

A bit later, Liz had been standing right behind him, waiting for a chance for a brief interview. He had been talking animatedly to one of his business partners and she had moved away, thinking she'd come back later, but he had spotted her and, as she was having second thoughts about interviewing him, Bob Maynard had turned and looked straight at her. He had been well aware of the pretty journalist who was busily writing in her notebook and suddenly he had strode across the room and was standing right in front of her, glaring and bristling with anger.

'Just what are you writing about, young woman?' he barked at her.

Liz had jumped back in surprise. 'Just an article for the *Bulletin*.' She tried to ignore his rudeness and smiled. 'Your daughter looks beautiful,' she added as she closed up her book and put it into her bag.

'Yes, well, I expect to get a copy of everything before it gets printed.' He had glared at her once more then turned and left.

Liz had felt shaken. How could people be so rude? What a disgusting, pompous little man. She felt sorry for Jenny having a father like that, and as for Jim the bridegroom, he was far from being a wimp, she thought. He must have been quite brave to have to put up with such a horrible father-in-law.

She had watched Maynard march across the room pulling a phone out of his pocket as he went through the French windows leading out to the patio.

Liz turned to greet Nancy, the mother of the bride, who was ready to talk about the trials and tribulations of arranging a wedding reception. It had apparently cost a small fortune. Then for the next ten minutes or so she had talked about catering, and her dress, and the bridesmaid's dresses and so on until Liz had far more information than she needed.

Eventually, she thanked Nancy for all the information and decided that now would be a good time to go upstairs to the powder room and freshen up. Afterwards, she had a bit of a wander around, admiring the portraits and stopped at the balcony overlooking the gardens. She had heard someone talking. They sounded as though they were having an argument and she leaned over to have a look.

It was Bob Maynard, and he was shouting at someone on the other end of the phone. 'Just give me the address,' Liz heard him say, and she quickly moved back, just as he glanced upwards. She didn't know whether he had seen her or not and, as she had hurried back down to the main room, decided that she had more than enough material for her column and that it was time to go. She didn't want to chance another encounter with Maynard. Her photographer, Jack, had already been, and left earlier. He had taken as many pictures as he wanted and they had chatted for a bit.

'See you Monday,' he had said.

Liz was thinking about all this now as she wrote the article while it was still fresh in her mind. It was an easy piece to do, one of many she had covered over the past six months. She gave a bit of a sigh, thinking about the wedding and especially about Bob Maynard, deciding not to mention anything about him which he possibly take offence to, then finished the piece for her column, read it through once again and pressed Send on the computer. She wondered if the editor would be sending it to Maynard for his approval before printing.

Next day was Sunday, and a bright spring day, so Liz put on her trackie dacks and runners and headed down the road for a jog. She didn't notice the blue Mazda parked down the street a little way. If she had, she might have wondered whether it was the same car she had seen last evening but it didn't cross her mind.

Joe Collins saw her, though, and quickly stubbed out his cigarette. He had been sitting there most of the previous evening and had moved the car further away when he had seen her at the window. When her lights went out, he had gone home and had then been back again first thing this morning. He felt bad about this job. That bloke had not given any reason why he wanted Joe to break into her house and find a particular notebook. He had his suspicions, though. If this girl was a reporter, then she had probably written down something that he wouldn't want anyone else finding out about.

Joe was a small-time crook. Break and enter was his speciality. He was usually quite successful at it. Unfortunately for him, yesterday afternoon Bob Maynard had caught him the one time he had made the stupid mistake of assuming no one was at home. As he had been about to remove the fly screen on the bathroom window, he had suddenly felt a blow to the back of his head which sent him crashing to the ground knocking him unconscious. When he came to, he was tied up to a kitchen chair and Bob Maynard was standing over him.

'So you're awake.' His face was red with fury. 'What do you think you were doing? Did you think you could actually break into my house? What were you looking for?' He gave Joe a slap around his face. 'I should call the police.' He glared at him and starting pacing around the room.

Joe couldn't speak, He had been caught fair and square and he was wondering why indeed this bloke hadn't called the police. He was beginning to think that would have been a better proposition than being tied up like this. He was getting a bad feeling.

'Um…' Joe cleared his throat. 'Why am I tied up?'

Maynard had stopped pacing and sat down. Joe wished he would stay in one place. All of this getting up and down was making him nervous.

'Do you know who I am?' Maynard had asked him then.

Joe looked him over carefully. 'No idea, mate,' he had racked his brains trying to place this person who, he had a feeling, was maybe someone he should have recognised.

Maynard had relaxed a bit and sat back in the chair, folding his arms. 'Why did you try and break into my house then?'

'Because I thought no one was home and there are a lot of trees in the front.' Joe had decided that honesty was probably the best policy, if he had a hope of getting out of there.

Maynard was quiet for a moment then leaned forward. 'I'll make you a deal,' he said.

Joe's mind was racing. This was getting weird. He considered his position. There wasn't much option, considering he was tied up, his head hurt and he didn't really want to go to the cop shop again. So, 'OK,' he said, 'what's the deal?'

Maynard stood up and started pacing again. He seemed agitated and trying to make up his mind about something. So Joe had waited. He wriggled his hands against the rope which wound around the back of the chair. He was getting cramp. He wished this geezer would get on with it.

'OK.' Maynard seemed to have come to a decision and sat down. 'If you agree to a little proposition I'm about to make, I'll not report you to the police and let you go.'

Joe's mind was racing. 'Depends,' he said. He shook his arms. 'Untie me, and I'll think about it.'

'No! No thinking about it. What I'm about to ask you to do is well within your capabilities.'

'How do I know you won't call the coppers anyway?' Joe was anxious. 'And I still don't know who you are. Why would I do anything for you?' A light bulb had gone off in his head. 'Is it something illegal then? Something not legit?' Continuing his honesty policy – for the time being anyway – Joe carried on, 'I don't do bad stuff. Just break and enter, that's what I'm good at. Well, most of the time,' he added.

'Exactly. I just want you to do something that you're good at.'

Joe decided. He nodded. 'OK then, it's a deal. What do you want me to do?' He wriggled his arms again. 'Untie me. I'm getting cramp.'

Maynard stepped forward then and untied the rope.

Joe made to get up and Maynard had pushed him back down. 'Not so fast, fella,' he said. 'First of all, what's your name?'

'What's yours?' Joe was quick with his retort but Maynard looked as though he was about to slap him again and Joe braced himself. 'All right, all right,' he said. 'It's Joe Collins. Satisfied? What do you want me to do?'

'I want you to break into a house and retrieve a notebook.' Maynard had studied him, sure of himself, assuming this little crook would do anything to get himself off the hook.

'That's all? That's all you want me to do?' Joe was still nervous but now a little bit intrigued. 'What sort of a notebook?' he asked. 'And what's the address?'

'They wouldn't give me her address,' Maynard growled.

'Who wouldn't?' Joe asked, and Maynard held up a hand as Joe added the obvious question, 'How am I supposed to know where to go then?'

'The person in question is at the moment,' he looked at his watch, 'in the Old Manor House north of the city, where my daughter's wedding reception is taking place. This woman is a nosy reporter who works for the *Bulletin*. Her name is Elizabeth Longley. She's tall and dark and easy to spot. I want you to find out where she lives by any means you can, follow her home if necessary. Watch the house until you're sure it's empty and then do what you do best. The notebook has a red cover with some stupid stickers on it and a spiral binding. When you've found it, you will put it in this envelope,' he handed one to Joe, 'and put it in the letterbox of this house.' He glared menacingly. 'And if you read anything in the notebook or say a word to anyone else about this, I will find you. Understand?'

Joe said nothing and then jumped as Maynard shouted, 'Do you understand? If you're caught, then it will be on your head. After all –

who are the police going to believe?' he smirked, then went over to the window. 'Is that your blue car across the street?'

Joe, still unable to think of anything to say, nodded. Then he thought of something. 'What's the address of this place?' he asked. 'And what name shall I put on the envelope?'

Maynard looked scathingly at him. 'I would've thought you already knew that, seeing as how you were planning to rob me. It's 18 Elm Street, and you don't need to know my name. I'll be the only person checking the mailbox. Now get going.' Maynard stepped aside as Joe made for the door.

Joe couldn't wait to get out of the house, and crossed the road quickly to his car. He sat for a moment, wrestling with decisions. If he did this job, he could be caught, and anyway how was he supposed find a book which must be like hundreds of others and could be the wrong one anyway? He had no doubt this bloke was serious, maybe even a little crazy, and he still hadn't said who he was. But Joe was curious now, and wondered just what was going on. Anyway, he thought, better to get the job done and hope that would be the end of it.

He put the car into gear and drove away, slowly at first then speeding up as he made his way across town. He knew the Old Manor House. In fact, he had done a job there once. It had been easy. There had been a function on and he had smiled to himself as he wondered whether they had ever noticed that a silver cruet set had gone missing.

The celebrations were apparently starting to wind down as Joe drew into the car park. He had parked next to a taxi, who seemed to be waiting for a passenger, and the driver was outside, scanning the people as they left the building. Joe held his breath as a beautiful, tall, dark-haired girl had emerged from the big Old Manor House and walked down the steps, making for the taxi.

He couldn't believe his luck as he heard her call to the driver, 'Are you waiting for me? Liz Longley?'

'Yes, miss, here we are.' The Indian driver was opening the door for her as he said, 'You are going to the station?'

'That's right.' She jumped in and they were away.

Joe had to decide what to do. This could be a problem. He was thinking quickly. If she was going to get a train, how was he going to follow her? Joe was used to making quick decisions, so he decided to follow the taxi at a safe distance to the station. As soon as both vehicles came to a stop in the station car park, he had waited for a moment then jumped out, locked the car door, bought a ticket to the furthest train stop just in case she was going that far, and followed Liz onto the train.

It wasn't hard to pick her out from the crowd. She was, he decided, definitely gorgeous. He had found a spot where he could keep an eye on her, and then check which station they were at when she left.

The train stopped only two stations later at Broadtown, and Liz had made a quick exit. Joe had got off along with the other passengers and followed her to the car park, where she had got into a white Nissan and drove away.

At first, Joe thought, that's it. She could be going anywhere now. He could have taken one of the two taxis waiting for passengers and asked the driver to follow her car, but quickly dismissed that idea. It would be too risky. If there was trouble later on of any sort, he would be remembered. This was a small station and only a few other people had got off the train.

He had another thought, which he pondered on while waiting for another train to take him back to the station where his car was parked. Making a mental note of the name of the suburb where Liz lived, Joe devised a plan. It was simple really. He had a telephone book in his car. He had her name. He had the make of her car and he had the suburb where she lived.

It was nearly half an hour before the next train pulled up and another ten minutes after that before Joe had got back to his car. He pulled his phone directory out from under the seat, and found the Longleys – there were only ten of them. There was only one E.J. Longley and that was at number 13 Broadview Street, Broadtown.

It couldn't be anyone else, he decided. On the little notepad he kept in the glovebox, Joe wrote down all the details, including the mobile phone number, shoved the phone book back under the seat, and got going again.

It was still only about five p.m. and he stopped at Maccas for a hamburger, then looked again in his phone book. He was getting more curious by the minute. Joe rang the Manor House, the number was in the book, and asked the female on the other end who had booked it that day. 'Bob Maynard,' she had said helpfully. 'It was his daughter's wedding reception.' Joe was thinking again. Why, for instance, wasn't Maynard, if that was his name, at the reception for his daughter's wedding? How come he would be the only one checking the mailbox? Didn't he have any other family at home? Also, Joe was wandering why he wanted the reporter's notebook. What had she written about that he didn't want known?

He drove slowly back to Broadtown and cruised around until he found Liz's address, then he had parked across the road and settled in for a wait. He had to see if she lived alone, suss out the place, and pick the right time to pay a visit.

He had waited for a couple of hours, smoking and watching. Joe was patient; he was used to waiting. He was good at picking quiet neighbourhoods, and luckily, this was one. No one came outside to check out a parked car, there were no pedestrians except one dog walker who passed along the other side of the road.

He saw Liz come to the window once and then pull the blinds down. That confirmed he had the right house at least, and it didn't look as though she was going out again today. There was only one car in the driveway, so the chances were she lived alone. He had waited a while longer until it was beginning to get dark and then went home.

So here he was now, parked down the street a little way and across the road from Liz's house on a beautiful Sunday morning. He had picked up a newspaper to pass the time, and was prepared to settle in for a bit of a wait until she left the house. He also knew that it was quite likely she wouldn't go out today, in which case he would try again tomorrow when she would probably leave for work.

So it was with a jolt that Joe suddenly saw a movement in his rear-vision mirror. Liz had left the house and was coming towards him. She was adjusting earphones and passed his car without a second glance. He watched her as she jogged past, admiring the trim figure and trendy tracksuit, then saw her go out of sight as she turned left at the bottom of the street.

He wasted no time and was out of the car in a jiffy, across the road and through the gate, around to the back of the house, where he expected to see, and was not disappointed to find, a bathroom window half open. Joe was small, skinny and wiry and used to clambering through small spaces quietly, and it took barely a minute before he was through and into the house.

He listened, just in case there was another person there, but all was quiet. He pulled his gloves out of his pocket and put them on as he did a quick sweep of the house, locating the small second bedroom which she used as an office. There it was, on the desk beside the computer – a red spiral notebook with butterfly stickers on the front.

Joe remembered that mad geezer telling him not to look in it. But who was he kidding, he thought. Of course he was going to have a quick gander, just to see what all the fuss was about. So he opened it up, and started laughing. It was all written in shorthand. Joe had seen shorthand before. Back in the day, he had had a girlfriend who was a secretary and she learned how to do it. He didn't think people still used it, what with voice recorders and such, but still, he decided it must come in handy if you wanted to write something down quickly. He would like to bet that Maynard feller wouldn't have a clue and this was all for nothing.

He stuffed the book in his pocket and went through the rest of the house, noting a nice gold watch on the bedside table. He pushed aside the natural thought which crossed his mind and left the watch where it was. Joe had his principles. This Liz lady seemed like a normal nice person and she didn't need any hassle from that Maynard bloke. So he picked up a pen, found a scrap pad and wrote a note. Then he went out the front door, carefully locking it behind him, looked both ways on the road, where there was no one in sight, got back into his car and left.

Joe drove back to the house on Elm Street and, as he had been instructed, put the notebook into the brown envelope, which was really too small and he had to really wedge it in, then he put it into the letter box. He had parked a bit further down the road just in case some nosy parker was about.

There was no sign of any other cars, and the place seemed to be deserted. The house on one side had a FOR SALE notice up. The other side was a vacant lot, which was why he had picked this house to break into in the first place. This time, though, he noticed the uncared-for garden, and the weeds in the pavers. Also, he wondered where Maynard's car had been parked, as he was sure there had been no other vehicle there when he had left yesterday.

If that bloke was having a posh wedding, how come he couldn't afford a gardener, was the next thought that crossed his mind. Taking a chance, Joe quickly looked around, opened a side gate and went through to the back of the house for a quick look and discovered a big shed with a padlock on the door.

He went around the building. There were no windows, but by now Joe's curiosity had the better of him. Padlocks were no problem and getting out his little case of lock-picking instruments, which were his tools of trade, he had it open in under a minute.

Moving quickly now, he slid through the door and then stopped, blowing a silent whistle as he surveyed the bags of white powder, stacked on a bench and the rows of Chinese-looking flowerpots lined up on a table. Joe couldn't wait to get out of there fast enough. He relocked the padlock, glad that he had remembered to keep his gloves on, and as he was leaving, noticed that there was a back gate leading out onto a lane, where, he realised, Maynard must have parked his car.

Then he left. This was serious stuff and Joe didn't want to have anything more to do with it. He made straight for his unit, a couple of suburbs away, and started to pack. He always rented furnished property, and always paid a month in advance. Luckily, there was no lease involved, so he was able to leave at will. He left a note for the landlord with the next-door couple, who expressed their sympathy for his having to visit his sick mother in another state and wished him all the best.

Then Joe was gone. He knew how to cover his tracks; he'd had plenty of practice. He hoped that Liz would be all right, and that bastard Maynard got what was coming to him.

When Liz came home from her morning jog, she didn't notice anything amiss until she had showered, breakfasted and then gone to switch on her computer. She frowned as she realised her notebook wasn't there, and looked around the house, wondering where she had put it, before coming back to her desk and then noticed the scrap pad.

She picked it up. In block capitals someone had written, 'SORRY I TOOK YOUR BOOK WATCH OUT FOR MAYNARD HES GOT IT IN FOR YOU 18 ELM ST. BURN THIS WHEN YOU HAVE RED IT.'

At first, Liz couldn't believe what she was reading. Then she realised someone had actually broken into her house. How? When? Then she knew how. Both doors were locked; it had to be through a window. Of course. She went into the bathroom. The window was half open. She sighed, she should have known better, but who'd have thought.

She felt shaky, angry, violated, knowing that some-one had actually been in her house. Her stomach churning, she went carefully back through the house to see if anything else was missing or disturbed, but everything seemed to be OK. Her handbag on the kitchen table was untouched, and her watch was still on the bedside table. She had nothing much of value to steal. Her computer was quite old.

She felt more angry about losing her notebook. Her beloved five-year-old niece Jessica had carefully put the butterfly stickers on the front of it when she had last visited. 'To remind you of me,' she had said, 'when you're doing your reporting.' So it was very special.

Liz sat down again, made a coffee and, feeling a little calmer now, reached for the phone to call the police, then she reread the cryptic note again and put the phone back down. OK, she thought, If I tell the police, they'll want to know how I knew Maynard was involved, which will mean showing them this note, which the writer wanted me to burn. And the thief must have some conscience, or he wouldn't have warned me.

She felt a little twinge of excitement. I could investigate this myself, she thought. My notes are all written in shorthand. No one could decipher it, of that she was certain. She had already sent off her piece for the *Bulletin*, and in any case there was nothing there that could be detrimental to Maynard. So why? What was he so worried about that he had to get someone to steal her book? Then she remembered the parked car the night before and a shiver went through her as she wondered if that had indeed been someone watching the house.

Suddenly, Liz jumped up and went to get her handbag. How could she have forgotten? Her little voice recorder was tucked inside, in the specially made pocket with a hole in it where she placed the machine with the microphone facing outwards, to catch any conversation which she thought might be useful in backing up any story she might be writing. She didn't use it all the time, because trying to record in a crowded room there was too much background noise and it was sometimes hard to pick up conversation very clearly, which was why Liz preferred to write her shorthand notes.

But sometimes she left it going and went through it afterwards to try and pick up anything she might have missed. Which was why she was feeling so excited now. She remembered she had switched it on upon arrival at the Manor House, and then just left it to record. It had been so noisy, what with all the music and people talking loudly enough to be heard, so she had just used her notebook.

The recorder had run out of space and stopped. Please let there be something, she thought as she pressed the Play button. At first, there was nothing but noise, general hubbub and no specific voices or conversation, and after about five minute' close listening, there seemed to be nothing she could pick out, but then she stopped the recorder and reversed it for a bit, then pressed Replay. Putting it close to her ear, she replayed a few times, before words gradually made sense.

Pretty sure it was Maynard speaking, she could only make out a few words, but it was enough to give her goosebumps. '…need to get down to Elm Street and check the…' then there was other noise and words she couldn't make out. Liz recalled standing behind him when he was talking to the other man. She hadn't been listening to the conversation, but it seemed the recorder had picked some of it up. She tried to remember what the other man looked like, but there was no recollection.

Liz replayed the rest but, apart from Nancy's rather loud voice talking about clothes and catering, there wasn't much else that was useful.

There was that address again. Elm Street. Liz knew that Maynard didn't live there. Nancy had talked about the mansion and the swimming pool at a beachside residence south of the town.

Liz knew now what she was going to do.

Bob Maynard had left it until late afternoon before going to check the mailbox. Nancy had not been happy at his leaving the reception early yesterday. She didn't know about the house in Elm Street and believed him when he explained how the property development business often meant he had to meet clients on a weekend, so she didn't complain too much. Her husband's work was what kept her in the manner to which she had become accustomed.

Maynard gave a grunt of satisfaction when he pulled the bulky package out of the mailbox. So that little crook had done it, then. He had half expected to find nothing. The book was wedged tightly inside the envelope, and in his haste he roughly ripped it open, retrieved the notebook and opened it. He turned the pages over with disbelief then proceeded to blaspheme loudly as he discovered it filled with shorthand.

He angrily stamped his way through the yard and around to the side of the house. Going through the backyard and out the rear gate to his car, he threw the notebook onto the back seat. Then he went to the shed, unlocked the padlock and checked inside. All was as it should be. Everything had to be packed up and ready for collection tonight. The others were scheduled to arrive this evening. He would be glad to get rid of this lot. The next delivery wasn't due for another week or so. In the meanwhile, he would have to decide what he was going to do about that reporter.

Liz drove slowly around the neighbourhood towards Elm Street. She had located it in her street directory and it was only about twenty minutes' drive from her home. It's lucky Maynard doesn't know what my car is like, she thought. She had dressed in jeans, a black T-shirt, tied her long dark hair back and pushed it under an old baseball cap, hoping she looked anonymous.

She cruised around the block and past Elm Street, noting the lane running along behind the houses parallel to the street. A car was there, parked up on the grass verge close to the fence, leaving space for any other vehicles to pass.

Then she stopped outside the house for sale, pretending to read the sign and write down the telephone number, just in case any neighbours were watching. It all seemed to be very quiet, and as she stood looking at the gate of number 18, undecided whether to risk taking a look around inside, she spotted something shiny glistening on the ground in front of the mailbox. Liz gave a gasp as she bent down to look more closely and saw a little yellow butterfly sticker. Quickly she rummaged in her pants pocket to find a crumpled tissue. Carefully she picked up the sticker, wrapped it in the tissue then went back to her car.

This was getting serious now. She had proof. The sticker had been torn off from the front of her notebook. Of that she was positive. So something dodgy was definitely going on, and she was not about to do any more investigating. There was one more thing she could do, though, and as she drove slowly past the end of the lane, she stopped long enough to write down the registration number of the car parked there, then headed for the nearest police station.

'I'd like to report a burglary,' Liz said to the young officer sitting at the desk.

'Name?' he asked, barely looking up.

'Elizabeth Longley.'

'Address?'

'13 Broadview Street, Broadtown.'

He glanced up, studied her. 'You're a local then?'

'Yes,' she said. 'Ssomeone broke into my house yesterday.'

'How did they get in?'

'Through the bathroom window'

He put his pen down. 'Were you in at the time?'

'No, I was out. Jogging,' she added.

'You realise that if you leave your window open then you're asking for trouble.'

She could see he was going to give a lecture on security. 'Yes, I know all about that,' she told him. 'Usually I would but this time I didn't. Anyway, it was a targeted robbery.'

'How do you know that?'

'He stole my notebook.'

'A notebook, that's all?'

'Yes, I'm a reporter and it was the notebook I use for interviews and things. Look, I think I need to speak to a detective.'

'You'd better come in to my office.'

Liz looked around at the person who spoken. DS Barry Johnston, who had been listening, was standing in the doorway behind her. He beckoned.

It was a quiet Sunday and he was having a break from catching up on paperwork. This could be interesting. 'Over here,' he said. 'I think we'd better have a bit of a chat.'

After she had sat where he indicated, she took off the baseball cap. It was too tight and uncomfortable and her hair tumbled out.

Barry Johnston looked up at her from a pad he had started to write on, said nothing for a moment, then asked her if she would like a coffee.

'That'd be great, thanks,' Liz smiled. 'White, no sugar.'

Barry spoke to someone on the phone, then put it down and studied her. 'I think you'd better start from the beginning. Elizabeth.'

'It's Liz,' she said.

'Right. Now, Liz, why would anyone want to steal your notebook?'

She sighed. 'I suppose I'd better tell you from the beginning.'

He smiled and nodded. 'It's a good place, and I'm a good listener.'

He has kind eyes, she thought, so she told him. All of it. About the reception. About Bob Maynard, and about the note the thief had left for her.

DS Johnston was looking more interested by the minute. 'Have you still got the note?' he asked.

She pulled it out of her bag and showed him. Then while he was carefully studying it, she told him about the voice recorder, going to the house, and about the butterfly sticker.

He looked up then. 'You do realise you should have made a report as soon as you realised your house had been broken into, and also it was damn stupid to go there on your own. Who knows what sort of trouble you could have got in.'

'I know that now,' she said. 'But look, if I hadn't gone over there, I wouldn't have found the sticker that must have come loose from my book. So that's proof, isn't it?'

He said nothing, just looked sternly at her.

'Well, I wouldn't have, would I?' she repeated.

DS Johnson called, 'Come in,' as someone knocked on his door, bringing two cups of coffee.

Liz put the butterfly sticker in the tissue in front of him on the desk, and then handed him a piece of paper. 'And here's the number of the car parked in the back lane. Which is still probably there,' she added. Then she took out the recorder. 'And here's the bit of conversation I recorded. I'm sorry it's not very clear.' She handed it to Barry, who, she thought smugly, was looking quite impressed.

He jumped up. 'Wait here.' And he hurried out of the office.

So Liz waited, sipping her surprisingly good coffee.

DS Johnston came back after about five minutes. He sat down looking very pleased with himself. He sat for a moment, debating, wondering just how much he should tell her. Then he decided she had a right to some answers considering all the information she had handed him.

'Well, for starters,' he said, 'you should know that we've had an eye on Maynard for some time, but nothing concrete has ever been proved. So thanks to your information and backing a hunch, I've sent a patrol car around to Elm Street to do some checking up.' Barry sat back and crossed him arms. 'That's all I can tell you at the moment, but I can say this time I hope we've caught him with the goods.'

Liz smiled happily, 'So will you let me know what happens?'

'Let me have your phone number,' he said, 'and I promise I'll be in touch.'

'And will it be all right if I write a report for the *Bulletin?*' she asked him. Then added, 'And can it be an exclusive? I mean, before any of the other newspapers get to know about it. That's if of course you get an…um…an arrest?'

'Once we've got it wrapped up, I don't see why not. The thing is, the TV stations always seem to get a hold of things of this nature, especially when it involves a public figure. Do you have a column, or a byline, or whatever?' he asked.

'No,' Liz replied sadly, 'at the moment I'm just doing weddings and funerals and stuff, but I want to prove to my editor I can do something more challenging.'

Barry smiled at her. 'Your editor at the *Bulletin* – Ollie Jackson, isn't it?'

Liz nodded.

'He plays golf with my dad. I'll make sure he knows what a good reporter he has on his staff.' He rose from the desk and held out his hand. 'I'll be in touch.'

Liz went home, pleased with herself, and started writing an account of everything that had happened, ready to give it to Ollie as soon as she got the OK from DS Johnston. It wouldn't matter, she decided, being a bit philosophical, if the TV stations got hold of the story first. Sometimes the journey was more interesting than the outcome.

Next day the promised phone call from DS Johnston came, asking her to call in at the police station. She went along after work, wondering why she was needed, what had happened.

'Sit down, Liz.' He was waiting for her and, as she sat down, she saw her notebook on his desk.

'Oh,' Liz exclaimed happily, 'my book, you've got it back.' She clasped it close. 'Where was it?'

'In his car,' he replied. 'Maynard's rego checked out and, as luck would have it, his accomplices were picked up a short time later. The officers found drugs being packed into fake Chinese vases. All in all, a good result. Thanks mainly to you, Liz. Plus,' he added, 'Maynard's fingerprints were on your notepad. So that wrapped it up nicely. The only thing we don't know is who actually did the break-in at your place. We could do a fingerprint search, but the chances are he used gloves if he was a professional. Would that be a problem for you?'

Liz thought for a quick moment then shook her head. 'I'm not going to worry about him any more. He may be a thief, whoever he was, but he had a conscience. He didn't have to leave me that note, did he, so no, I feel no threat whatsoever. I don't expect he'll be back.'

So it was a good result. Maynard went to jail, his wife had to get used to living the way she had been unaccustomed, Ollie was so impressed with Liz's account of her weekend's detective work that he promoted her to junior crime reporter on probation for three months. DS Johnston was getting up the courage to ask Liz for a date, the yellow butterfly was more firmly glued in place where it belonged on the front of her notebook, and as for Joe Collins, he was tempted to phone up Liz and ask how it all panned out but he never did.

Connecting the Dots

'Who's that?'

'She's the substitute teacher.'

'Where's the usual one, then?'

'Dunno. Maybe she's sick or something.'

'I don't like the look of this one.'

'Why?'

'She looks weird.'

'Why weird?'

'Well, for starters, she's wearing a skirt.'

'There's nothing wrong with a skirt. She's a sheila.'

'Yeah, I know that, but what about the class? It's supposed to be phys. ed.'

'So?'

'How's she going to do phys. ed. in a skirt?'

'Dunno. Maybe it's not going to be phys. ed.'

Margery Simpson had heard all the small talk going on and was used to it. She was more than ready for this class of thirteen-year-olds. They were from the rough end of town. She had noticed the odd haircuts and ear piercings and the loud comments. Margery, however, had her own quiet way of dealing with undisciplined rowdy kids.

She plonked both feet firmly on the floor and drew herself up to her full height, which even then was shorter than most of the students. She pushed big dark spectacles up on her nose and regarded her class.'

'Everyone take your seats.' Her voice belied her small stature. It had the sound of authority and rang out loud and clear as she looked at people who were still milling around.

She waited, not moving and not saying another word, as the class gradually quietened and they all eventually settled down.

'Mr Parker's away sick today,' she announced. 'I am your substitute teacher Miss Simpson, and instead of doing phys. ed. you'll be doing something a little different.'

There were murmurs of disquiet, and a few groans as the class showed their displeasure. Most of them enjoyed the physical education class. It got them away from the work that required concentration like maths or science.

'So what are we going to do then, miss?' A voice from the back of the class held a note of wariness as though they were going to be asked to do something completely out of their comfort zone.

'Yeah, like what?' another voice rang out, sounding sarcastic, prepared to scorn and belittle anything this unwanted substitute teacher might come up with.

Instead of replying, Margery went to the blackboard which ran along the wall in front of the classroom. Taking up a piece of chalk, she did a big scribble of no particular design – scrolls and swirls, circles and squares. Then, facing the class, who were gazing at the scribbles in stunned silence, she took a pile of large sheets of plain paper from her desk and handed it to a boy sitting in front. 'Hand this around, please,' she said.

When they had all got their paper, the class waited, chattering again, wondering what they were supposed to do now.

A lone voice whispered loudly, 'What's all this crap, then?' but was shushed by a girl from behind, and the class quietened as they waited now, expectant.

'What do you see?' Margery indicated the blackboard.

Nobody responded for a minute, then 'A great big mess, miss,' came from the third row and there were a few titters.

'Exactly.' Margery agreed. 'A big mess.' Then she took up a piece of chalk and, using some of the squiggles and circles, started filling in the spaces, adding straight lines, shading and blocking. Gradually a picture began to emerge and the random marks on the board slowly turned into a drawing of a garden with trees and a little shed.

Margery turned back to the class, who hadn't moved from their seats. They were now all gazing at the board and the room was strangely quiet.

'That's cool,' she heard a whisper.

'Now I'd like you to get your pencils out,' she held up her hand as a few arms shot up, 'and all those of you who didn't bring pencils today, I have spare ones, so come and get one, plus you'll need an eraser. You'll find everything in that box.' She indicated a box on her desk and waited.

Eventually, half a dozen of the boys left their desks and somewhat reluctantly came forward and helped themselves. She noticed that all of the girls had already taken out their pencil cases and were looking interested. There were fifteen in her class – ten boys and five girls. Most of them were in the 'too hard basket', according to Matt Parker. He managed to control them with threats and promises of dire consequences if they didn't behave. In his opinion, they would probably all leave school without finishing their education and go on the dole.

Margery was an optimist. She had a simple philosophy. Respect breeds respect. Sometimes it worked and sometimes it didn't. She waited now until they were all settled again.

'Now I'd like you to do just what I did. Draw a random sketch taking any form you like on your paper. It can be as much or as little as you like. Whatever marks you make must be done quickly. I don't want you to think too much about it. Just do it. You can close your eyes if you like. Don't take more than thirty seconds. You can start…' she waited for a few seconds as they all took up their pencils, '…now!'

One by one, they started to do their scribbles, some enthusiastically, some reluctantly. Some raised their faces to her in puzzlement, one boy in the front rolled his eyes with absolute scorn, but still he then turned to his paper and started to draw.

'OK.' Margery glanced at her watch. 'Time's up. Everybody finished?'

There were some nods.

'Right. Good. Now, I want you to have a good look at what you've done. And then, using the marks you have already made, using all or some of your sketch, you may attempt to turn them into a picture, as I have done.' She indicated the board. 'I don't expect a garden,' she added. 'That was just to demonstrate what's possible. It can be something quite simple – a butterfly, an animal, a tree, anything at all.' She looked around the class. 'It could even be a feeling. Think about it, and use your imagination.'

She waited for any comments, but there were none. So she continued, 'This is not a competition. There is no best, or worst, there will be no marks. This is something for you, not me, just you.' Margery looked at her watch. 'You have twenty-five minutes.'

Then she went and sat behind her desk and waited. She regarded her class. As she had expected, there were a few moans and savage mutterings, and she could see that some of them were going to have trouble getting started. So she stood up again. 'If you're having a problem getting started, then sometimes it helps if you turn your sketch upside down or sideways, and look from another angle,' she remarked.

Immediately some of them did just that. Gradually they settled down; the scowls disappeared as they warmed to their task.

One of the girls raised her hand. 'Miss?'

'Yes?' Margery smiled.

'Can I use my coloured pencils?'

'Certainly.' She looked around. 'If any of you have coloured pencils, you may use them.'

Twenty-five minutes passed quickly and then Margery stood up again. 'Pencils down, everyone.'

A couple of the girls kept drawing for a few moments. Some of the others were holding their pictures up, showing their neighbours, looking quite surprised at the results. She watched their faces and to her satisfaction saw some reluctant signs of pride.

Margery decided that twenty-five minutes of silence in this class deserved praise. 'Well done,' she said.

She checked the time. They had five minutes before recess. They were all chattering again.

'Would anyone like to come forward and show their picture?' Margery asked them now. 'It's only if you'd like to share with the class. You don't have to.'

She waited. Then a raised arm. One of the girls.

'Yes, good. What's your name?'

'Lisa Jones,' the girl replied.

Margery beckoned. 'Thank you, Lisa.'

The girl came forward, holding her picture carefully. Margery nodded her encouragement.

'This is a picture of some daises.' Lisa spoke softly. She held it up.

It was indeed a fairly good rendering of some flowers that could have been anything. But Lisa was obviously proud of her work and Margery beamed at her.

'That's lovely, Lisa. Well done.'

Then another girl came up and showed her picture of a cat, using her coloured pencils, which was remarkably good.

The boy from the front who had complained the most came forward and held his picture high. 'This is lightning,' he said with a smirk.

There were zigzags all over the picture and Margery could see that he had taken very little trouble with embellishing the zigzags he had made on his original sketch. He had thought he was being very smart, and waited for some comment to that effect from Margery, but instead she was high in her praise.

'Well done, Jack,' she said. 'You have a good imagination.'

One by one, they ventured forward to show their work. There were some imaginative drawings, some bizarre. There were stick men, clowns, clouds, even a dinosaur.

Margery made sure that everyone got a word of praise or encouragement. She had a feeling that this class of students rarely got praised for anything very often.

When they were done, although only about two-thirds of the class had come forward with their pictures, Margery was more than satisfied. At least they had all had a go.

'You may all keep your pictures,' she said, 'but before you go,. I would like to know what you think you've learned today.' She waited. 'Anyone?'

A hand went up.

'Yes? Sally, isn't it?'

'Well, I think I learned that even if there's a big mess, then you can always find something…um…you didn't expect if you try hard enough.'

Margery gave one of her beaming smiles. 'Most definitely,' she said. 'Well done, Sally.'

Another voice came out of the middle. 'Yeah, and sometimes you just have to join the dots to get the picture.'

Unexpectedly, they all laughed and clapped just as the bell rang for recess.

After the room had emptied, Margery walked around the desks. All of the class had taken their pictures with them with the exception of the one with zigzags. The boy – Jack, she thought it was – had left his behind.

Easter Weekend

Percy Potter didn't pay much attention to public holidays. In the retirement village where he lived, one day tended to blend in with the next. So when someone reminded him that next weekend was Easter, he knew that it would be just the same as usual. For Percy, there would be no family trip away. His daughter and her family had moved interstate for her husband's job six months ago and he didn't get to see them very often.

'Are you going to be OK, Dad?' she had asked him. Worried. 'We can always keep in touch with the emails and you must promise you'll phone me if there are any problems.'

Of course he had reassured her. He would be fine, he said. He had help on call if he needed it, and anyway he was fit as a fiddle. Plus he liked it here, he had told her, and he was quite happy. and she was not to worry.

People talked excitedly about going to the races, or the beach or to the relations for the weekend and when they called out, 'Have a good weekend, Percy' or 'Happy Easter,' he said, 'Thank you. You too,' and smiled.

Percy went for his usual walk, watched a DVD he'd borrowed from the library and checked his emails. There was one from his granddaughter Sarah, who wished him a happy Easter and told him how they were going camping for the weekend. She was ten now and sometimes sent him emails. He looked forward to those letters and always answered, though sometimes it was difficult to know what to say that was interesting enough to write about.

Thursday evening, Percy cooked his dinner, read his book and turned the TV on and had his usual quiet night in. Next morning when he went for his walk, there was hardly anyone about, no one to say g'day to or have a chat, so he decided to drop in at the village coffee shop, but stopped short when he saw the closed sign. He frowned, then realised of course it was closed for Good Friday. How could he have forgotten?

Percy walked back home feeling a little bit disgruntled and reluctantly admitted to himself he felt a bit lonely. A new feeling for him. He had got used to being alone, but comfortable in his skin, and not lonely.

It was a great day, nice autumn weather, so Percy collected his book and a bottle of water from the fridge and went outside. His house was at the end of the row which led into the community garden. It had been made comfortable and welcoming for the residents of the village, and Percy sat on his favourite bench seat under the big old pepper tree.

He was totally engrossed in the latest Tim Winton novel, when a small voice pierced his consciousness.

'Hello. What's your name?'

Percy gave a little startled jump and looked up into the very blue eyes of a small girl about five years old. He hadn't seen her arrive, and looked around. There wasn't an adult in sight, so he put his book down and regarded the small person with a smile. 'Hello, young lady,' he said. 'Who are you?'

'I asked you first,' she replied.

'Well, so you did,' he said. 'Well, my name's Percy Potter. Now you can tell me yours.'

'It's Samantha Jane but Mummy and Daddy call me Sam.'

'OK, Sam it is. Now, Sam, where is your mummy?' It had been a long time since Percy had had a conversation with a small girl and he looked around, wrinkled concern on his face.

'She's visiting with Grandma.' Sam approached the bench. 'Can I sit here?'

Percy nodded and she climbed up onto the bench and made herself comfortable.

'Does your mum know where you are?' he asked her now, still concerned, but Sam nodded.

'Mummy said I could go outside but to stay close. She's over there.' Sam pointed to a house across the way two doors down.

Percy was puzzled. He had thought that house was empty. There again, he didn't really take much notice of the comings and goings of the neighbours. But he was little intrigued now. 'Has your grandma been there for a long time?' he asked.

'Yes, a long time.' Sam pondered. 'Two weeks. Grandma Rosie has a poorly leg,' she added.

'Poorly leg?'

'Yes, her leg doesn't work and she has a wheelchair.'

Percy was intrigued. He had most certainly never seen anyone in a wheelchair emerge from that house. 'Well, that's too bad,' was all he could manage.

'Well, that's too bad.' She parroted him, and he had to smile. 'But she doesn't use it,' Sam continued. 'She says she doesn't like it. She says that wheelchairs are for old people.' Sam looked up at him. 'But Grandma's old too, so she should use it, shouldn't she?'

Percy didn't answer. Couldn't. When you're old, you forget you're old. You look around at other old people and you know you're not like them. He totally understood how Sam's grandmother felt. He was pondering this when she jumped down from the bench.

'Oh, look, there's Mummy,' her voice rose with excitement, 'and look, she's got the wheelchair and Grandma's in it.' She ran towards them.

'Where were you, Sam?' A nice-looking young woman with the same blonde hair and blue eyes as her daughter was adjusting the footrest of a wheelchair, and the elderly lady sitting in it with one leg covered in plaster looked cross and uncomfortable.

'I've been talking to Mr Percy,' Sam said as the wheelchair approached his seat.

Percy stood up. 'G'day,' he smiled. 'Young Sam's been keeping me company.'

The young woman put out her hand. 'How do you do, Mr Percy,' she said. 'Nice to meet you. I'm Jan. I hope my daughter hasn't been bothering you. She is a bit of a chatterbox.' She smiled and nodded towards her mother, 'And this is Mary, Sam's grandma.'

Mary looked up at Percy and saw a rather shy smile, a distinct twinkle in grey eyes almost invisible under bushy grey eyebrows which were shadowed under a blue baseball cap matching the colour of his T-shirt.

'G'day.' Percy put out his hand, 'I see you've got wheels,' he said. He made it sound as though she was privileged and lucky. 'I could do with some of those myself.' He clasped his back. 'This gives me gyp sometimes.'

Jan looked at her watch. 'We'll have to go, Mum, or we'll miss the train.' She looked down at her mother. 'Will you be OK?' She glanced at Percy, who got the message.

'Don't you worry,' he said. 'I'll make sure she gets back OK. In fact, I'll be glad of something to hang on to.' He went over and grabbed the handles of the wheelchair. 'Would you like to take a turn around the garden, madam?' he asked in his poshest voice.

Mary laughed. 'Thank you, kind sir,' she said. 'That would be lovely.'

Sam gave her grandma a hug. 'See you next time, Grandma. Mr Percy's going to look after you, aren't you, Mr Percy?'

'It'll be a pleasure,' he said, and indeed it was.

The next day, the village shop was open again and Percy bought an Easter egg then went and presented it to Mary.

'Happy Easter,' he said.

Holy Eggs

The two eggs sat side by side in specially made cups on a bed of black velvet. This was placed on a beautifully carved wooden altar-like structure set into a niche, which had been hollowed out in the stone in the back wall of the cave. A glass dome covered the top of the eggs to keep prying, grubby hands away from the precious relics. Candles were glowing in other hollows of the cave and there was a hush among the visiting tourists who spoke in whispers.

For years now, many people had been making a pilgrimage to the caves near the village to pay homage to the Holy Eggs, and this had brought prosperity to the hitherto poor people of the area. Shops had opened which had been closed for a long time. Cafés appeared and food stalls set up to provide sustenance to people who had been queuing for hours, just to get a glimpse of the remarkable ancient artefacts.

The Holy Eggs were two different colours. One green, the colour of the stunted shrubs struggling to grow in the poor sandy soil of the area, and the other ochre, the colour of the earth. There was a jagged hole in the top of each egg and they had a rough exterior with small lumps protruding on the outside like warts, giving them an odd appearance.

The legend was that the extraordinary and strange creatures that had emerged from the Eggs thousands of years ago were not of this world. They were said to have had brightly coloured wings and human-like heads and could be seen glowing with a radiant phosphorescent light.

There had been reports of people seeing them flitting among the trees at night but pictures of these beings had never been taken. They were said to disappear in a flash of light as soon as a camera was pointed at them. Be that as it may, there was no doubt that there were many pictures of them painted on the walls of the caves, and this confirmed to the excited tourists that these beings had actually existed, and maybe still exist today. Unfortunately, no photographs were allowed to be taken in the caves, as the flashes were said to damage the relics.

The Holy Eggs had magical healing powers and indeed, sometimes people who had been kneeling in homage had risen to their feet exclaiming in wonder, 'My back is healed,' they cried. A woman who was blind claimed to be able to see again and a small crippled boy regained the use of his legs and walked away from his wheelchair accompanied by his mother, who was wailing with joy.

The stories of the Eggs became legend which changed according to the person relating the tale. Some thought there was a religious significance and that the hand of God was involved in some way, although to what purpose no one could quite decide.

There were of course some sceptics who questioned the authenticity of the Holy Eggs. In fact, one young person was heard to remark that perhaps they were called Holy Eggs because there was a hole in them. She was chided for such irreverence and told in no uncertain manner to remove herself from the cave.

One of the storytellers was an elderly gentleman called Matthias, who had had lived in the village all of his life, and his shop, which sold objects, artefacts and curios for the tourists, had prospered. He talked about the magical properties of the Holy Eggs, and how they came to be discovered by geologists who were excavating for fossils. His voice was deep and full of reverence and the people listened to every word. He told them that he had lived such a long healthy life because he visited the Eggs every day. He was, he said, Keeper of the Eggs and was entrusted to make sure they were always kept safe, which he had always done, and one day he would pass on this special task to one of his sons or grandsons.

Matthias had two sons and two daughters who had married and produced children and grandchildren, who now attended the village school which, thanks to the money flowing into the village, had modern classrooms and equipment. One of the teachers was a young Australian called Josh, who was travelling around the world earning a living from teaching and his speciality was art and crafts..

It was coming up to Easter time and Josh decided that his class of ten-year-olds should make some Easter eggs. He asked the children to bring some chicken eggs to school (as most of the families kept chickens, this was not a big ask) and he showed them how to make small holes and blow out the insides. He provided them all with glue, paint, feathers, bits of grass and so on and said they could decorate their eggs however they liked. The children set to with enthusiasm. Of course some eggs were broken and were replaced, but all in all they did some excellent work and they took their eggs home, proud of their achievements.

Matthias's great grandson, Peter, showed him his decorated egg. 'Look what I made, Grandfather,' he said. 'Are you proud of me?'

Matthias patted Peter's head. 'Indeed you have done remarkably well,' he praised him, 'and I am very proud of you.'

After Peter had left, carefully holding his precious egg, Matthias was deep in thought for a while. Then he made his way down into the cellar. This was his place. No one was permitted to enter. It was where he kept objects, artefacts and curios and so on that he sold in his shop. Many things were handmade; the woodcarvings especially were exquisite.

He walked over to the back corner where it was darker and lit a couple of candles. There upon a shelf were twelve large chicken eggs. Some were painted in green and some in ochre. Four were unpainted but all had a small jagged hole in the top. There was also some glue next to a bowl of tiny seeds ready to be used.

Matthias carefully picked up one of the eggs that was finished. He was pleased with it. Soon it would be time for the yearly swap over before the deterioration started to show. He smiled to himself. Now that Peter had showed such promise, he knew that one day when he felt it was time, he would have a worthy successor to pass on his job as Keeper of the Holy Eggs.

Road Signs

Jenny Thomas stamped her foot on the brake as the STOP sign suddenly loomed out of the darkness, illuminated by the headlights.

She switched on the inside light and peered closely at the GPS. The American-accented voice had gone quiet. The last direction she had been given was to turn left at the next intersection, which she had attempted to do, but the sign was planted squarely in the middle of the road. It was one of those portable ones commonly used by road workers, and Jenny was momentarily at a loss.

'116 Madison Street,' she repeated loudly. But the GPS was silent. So Jenny rummaged in the glovebox to find a torch and got out of the car. She shone it around and located the street sign on the corner pointing along the road. Madison Street, it said.

So at least I'm at the right place, she thought. She frowned as she shone the light along the road. There didn't appear to be any obstructions, the road was clear of any roadworks.

'Someone having a joke,' she muttered, and shoving the torch in her coat pocket, she bent over the offending sign and, half lifting it, dragged it across the road and dropped it into the dirt on the verge.

Climbing back into the car, Jenny put it into gear, and cautiously started to drive along Madison Street. She was new to this part of town, having only lived in the area for a couple of months, so it was unfamiliar territory and out in the countryside.

'It's easy to find,' Grace had told her. 'just half an hour's drive from here.'

She was wondering whether her decision to join the book club had been such a good idea. She had met Grace and Henry at her friend

Anne's book launch, and Jenny had enjoyed listening to the speeches, partaking of the wine and refreshments, and mingling with the other book lovers who had been there. She had blushed when Anne had publicly thanked Jenny for giving her the confidence she needed to get her book of poems published.

Jenny had never met Grace and Henry before, but assumed they were invited guests and friends of Anne. So when they approached her and asked if she would be interested in joining a book club, she was tempted. She loved to read and thought a book club would be fun and maybe she would find some like-minded friends. So she had agreed, although there was a moment's doubt when she asked Anne about the couple and her friend had shook her head.

'No, I don't know them,' she had told her, 'but there again, there were quite a few people at the launch who I didn't know.' She had laughed. 'Some people just like to go to book launches. It's not a secret and it's free, but you have to wonder if they just go for the food and drinks.' She gave Jenny a hug. 'You should go, you'd enjoy it, and it's time you went out a bit more. In fact,' she added, 'I'd come along too, but I'll be away for the next couple of weeks, I'm off to Perth on the weekend to visit family. So I'll see you when I get back and you can tell me all about it.' She smiled. 'Aand thanks again, Jen. I'd never have given this publishing business a go if not for your continual nagging. And guess what?'

'What?

'I sold thirty books,' she had said happily.

Jenny pondered on this and wished her friend was with her. She also wished she had left home earlier, it seemed to have gotten dark so quickly. She hoped she had written the address down correctly, realising she should have asked for a phone number to call in case she couldn't find the right house. But she always relied on the GPS, although if that malfunctioned, she thought now, she'd be in strife.

Slowly she drove along Madison Street trying to make out the house numbers, which was difficult because some had no numbers.

The houses all seemed to be well back from the front, which had high untidy bushy fences. She finally located a number 21 on a letter box on the right hand side. So number 116 would have to be on the left, she decided, and much further along.

Suddenly, there was another sign right in the middle of the road again. WRONG WAY GO BACK. Luckily she was driving slowly and Jenny stopped again. She looked at her watch. Seven fifteen. The meeting started at seven thirty. If I don't get there soon, I'll be late, she thought. She felt a little panicky. She hated being late for anything and this was getting ridiculous.

Feeling annoyed now, she almost did a U-turn there and then, to return home, but she was also becoming curious. What was going on?

Suddenly making a decision, she got out of the car again and heaved the sign onto the side of the road. I'll give it one more shot, she muttered.

It was very dark now, and cold. But there was a full moon, giving some light, although it disappeared every time a cloud passed over. Jenny realised that there were no street lights. She looked in the rear-vision mirror. There was just one light she could see way back behind her. She glanced towards the house where she had stopped. There were no lights coming from it and there were no lights in the house across the road either. Then with a shock, she realised she hadn't seen any lights at all coming from any houses since she had turned the corner into Madison Street.

She started the car again, undecided now, feeling a little spooked, and crept slowly ahead. Suddenly she spotted a house number attached to an old rusty letter box. She wound the window down and shone her torch. 114, it said, although the number 4 was hanging off sideways. Just then the moon became free of cloud and she could get a better look at the house. There was a broken gate and she could see along a pathway to a pile of debris and the remains of a large structure which could have been a house once upon a time.

Well, it's got to be the one next door then, Jenny thought, as she drove carefully to the next house and stopped. She got out of the car, shining her torch on what would have once been a fence, but it was now almost completely wrecked. She found an old tin sign lying on the ground. The number 116 had almost disappeared but she could still make it out. Jenny went up to the big gap in the ruins of the broken fence and shone her torch light towards the house. Only there wasn't a house. Just a pile of bricks, a few window frames still attached, and a tiled roof complexly collapsed onto the lot.

That did it. Thoroughly unnerved now, Jenny turned towards the end of the road. There was another sign. DEAD END. And there was a roughly spray-painted skull and crossbones alongside it. Behind the sign was a barbed wire fence stretched right across the road in front of a paddock, which as far as Jenny could see had nothing but a few straggly trees. But it was so dark that in spite of the moon it was difficult to see much else.

She was aware of the quiet. No cars, no lights, no signs of life, not even a barking dog. Jenny shivered and got back into the car, turned up the heater, did a U-turn and headed back along Madison Street.

Just as she reached the junction, the GPS came back to life, so Jenny told it her home address. 'Turn right,' it said.

Monday morning and back at work in the local council office, Jenny related her experience to Jock Mackie, who had worked there for years and was a bit of a history buff.

He looked at Jenny over his glasses. 'Madison Street. You went to Madison Street?

She nodded. 'I think I must have had the wrong address.'

'I should think you did,' he laughed. 'You wouldn't have got much joy there. It's been taken over by developers and all the old houses are being knocked down. Nobody lives there any more. It was all because of the fire,' he added.

'Fire?'

'A couple of years ago. Of course you were still in Queensland then, weren't you? Maybe you didn't hear about it. Anyway, there was a bushfire, tore across the paddock and into most of Madison Street. Very bad it was. Some people couldn't get away in time. They do say the worst hit were some folks who used to have a book club, up the end of the street.' He smiled. 'You'd better make sure you have the right address next time.'

'Yes,' she said. 'I think I'd better.'

Roses Are Red

Stanley Barber was very proud of his roses. They grew in neat rows across his front lawn in alternating colours. Pinks, reds yellows and white. They made a pretty pattern and indeed looked quite spectacular.

Much of Stanley's life was spent tending to his rose garden. He didn't have any other interests apart from being a member of the local gardening club which met once a month, where he was always happy to share information on the growing of roses with like-minded people.

He was sometimes asked to speak about his roses, so, assuming that no one knew half as much as he, he spoke at length about fertilising, pruning, cutting and so on. Sometimes he spoke for a very long time and was surprised that when he asked for questions, none were forthcoming. So he thought that people were too afraid to show their ignorance in front of everyone else, and didn't like to ask questions that would put them in a bad light in front of all the expert gardeners.

Stanley therefore kindly invited people to call and see him, which sometimes the new members of the gardening club did, then he would show them his roses and explain how it was all done. How he managed to get such amazing results.

They oohed and aahed and Stanley basked in their praise.

Sometimes he would stand near his front gate and watched for people as they came along the street, mostly dog walkers. He would hail them with a cheery 'Good morning.' Then they would stop and of course couldn't help admiring the garden.

Stanley would then launch forth about his roses, and could go on ad infinitum if not stopped by the person, who always seemed to be in a hurry to get somewhere else.

One of the people who stopped was a young man walking his dog on Sunday morning.

When Stanley called out 'Good morning,' Simon Jackson nearly tripped over his dog in surprise. He hadn't noticed the portly middle-aged man until he had drawn level with the gate.

'Morning,' Simon muttered in reply. He was walking his dog late today because he had been on the phone to his fiancée Jenny. They had had a fight over how many invitations they could manage for their upcoming nuptials. So Simon was upset and cranky. He didn't feel like chatting to this old bloke who had started going on about his roses.

Simon glanced over the fence at the garden. 'Yes, they're very nice,' he managed, then quickly walked on.

Stanley looked after the hastily departing body of Simon. 'Always in a hurry,' he muttered. 'Young people, don't even have time to stop and chat.'

That evening, Stanley was watching a gardening programme on TV and was so engrossed he forgot to check the CCTV which he had installed outside. If he had looked half an hour earlier, he would have seen someone in black clothes creeping around his garden. So it wasn't until the next morning when he went to do some watering that Stanley had the worst moment of his life.

He stopped in horror and fell against the side of the house. He couldn't believe his eyes. All of the red roses were gone. Shakily he got to his feet and went to check the others.

Yes – just the red ones. All twelve were gone. Stanley knew exactly how many blooms were on each bush. Whoever had done this thing hadn't even done a proper job. At least some of the buds had been left behind. And some had been cut much too close to the top.

All the others roses seemed to be untouched.

Stanley was so upset he couldn't bring himself to do the watering. He went back inside and sat down. He was completely bereft. It was like the feeling of loss he had when his dear wife Elsie had passed away ten years ago. In a way it was worse, because looking after the roses had been her passion to start with, and had become his obsession to keep them going in her memory.

He was feeling violated and incensed. He felt an anger he had never experienced before. How dare they? How dare they come into his garden and steal his roses? The red ones were the most loved. They were Elsie's favourites.

After he had calmed down a bit, Stanley decided to phone the local police station. 'I wish to report a theft,' he said.

'Yes, sir. May I have your name and address please?' The policeman spoke firmly and with an air of calm as befitted the situation of dealing with a person, sounding decidedly upset, who had experienced the trauma of being robbed.

Stanley gave his name and address and then was asked, 'What has been stolen, Mr Barber?'

'My roses.'

'Roses?'

'Yes, twelve of my best prize roses. Red ones.'

'I see, sir. And when did this happen?'

'Last night,'

'And when did you discover your roses had gone?'

'This morning of course.' Stanley was getting impatient. 'So what are you going to do about it?'

'I'll make a report and a police officer will call to see you and take all the details.' The policeman sounded a little less calm.

'When?'

'I'm sorry, sir. I can't give you a time. All of our police officers are out attending to other priorities. But someone will come as soon as possible.

'That's not good enough!'

'I'm sorry, sir, that's the best I can do at the moment.'

Stanley gave a disgusted grunt and disconnected the phone. Then he waited for the rest of the day with increasing impatience for a policeman to call. He had heard sirens approaching on a couple of occasions but the police cars went straight past and he stayed up nearly all night watching his CCTV, but nothing untoward happened.

The following morning, Stanley was almost resigned to the fact that nothing was going to be done about the theft. So he was quite surprised when around eleven am there was a knock on the door and a young policewoman stood there. She had been admiring the garden and turned when Stanley opened his door.

'Good morning, are you Mr Barber?'

Stanley nodded. 'Come in.' He stood back. 'I suppose you've come about the robbery?'

She nodded and glanced behind her, indicating the garden. 'I understand some of your roses have been taken.'

Stanley led the policewoman through to his lounge room and indicated a seat. 'Well,' he started in a slightly accusing tone, 'What have you found out. Have you discovered the culprit?'

Joanne Batts had studied psychology and set about reassuring Stanley without him becoming aggressive. 'Mr Barber,' she started, 'you must understand that the theft of flowers is a fairly common occurrence, and the hope of catching the culprit is quite difficult unless of course they're caught in the act.' She glanced at Stanley, who was glaring at her.

'Isn't that what the police are for? To catch criminals. Those roses were part of my prize-winning selection. Whoever took them must have known they were valuable and did it to spite me.'

'Do you know anyone who would want to make mischief for you? Has this happened before?'

'No, I don't,' Stanley admitted. 'No one I know would even think of doing such a thing.'

'Then,' Joanne said, 'it looks as though it was just an impulsive thing. Someone thought your roses were so beautiful they couldn't resist. The likelihood of catching them is very remote. I'm sorry, Mr Barber,' she added, 'but really there's very little we can do. We can keep track of any other similar thefts in the neighbourhood, but so far nothing else has been reported.' She watched Stanley as his demeanour changed from hostile to dejection and she felt sorry for him. She had an idea. 'Mr Barber,' she said, 'do you know a lot about roses?'

'Of course I do.' He studied her. 'Why do you ask?'

'Would you like to give a talk about, well, growing them and how to cultivate them and things like that?'

'Yes, I give talks at my gardening club.'

'Well,' Joanne continued, 'I have a friend who volunteers at the Helping Hand Community Centre and they're always looking for guest speakers. Would you be interested in giving a talk at one of their meetings? They're mostly retired folks and are really into gardens.' She looked at Stanley, who had started looking interested.

'Well, I suppose I could.'

'There would also, I believe, be a small remuneration in appreciation.' Joanne looked hopefully at Stanley, who appeared to be deep in thought. He had never spoken at any other function apart from his gardening club where everyone knew him.

He made up his mind. 'Yes, all right, I'll do it.' His mind was racing now. He had so much knowledge to impart about the cultivation of roses. This was indeed something he could do.

'That's great.' Joanne smiled. 'I have your number so I'll give you a call and,' she added, 'I'm so sorry about your roses.'

After she had gone, Stanley found himself thinking about what he would say at the meeting and proceeded to draw up a list of topics he could talk about. For a little while, he forgot about the theft.

The arrangements were made and two weeks later Stanley presented himself at the Helping Hand Community Centre. He was greeted enthusiastically by the members, who after listening to him for twenty minutes – luckily a time limit had been stipulated – gave an overwhelming round of applause, much to Stanley's satisfaction, and to top it off he was asked to come back.

An excellent afternoon tea was served and then the guest speaker for the following month was announced. A bee-keeper who was to talk about his bees, hives and the extraction of honey. Stanley was asked if he would like to attend and he said that yes, he would.

That night for the first time since the theft he didn't worry about someone stealing his roses. He thought instead of the upcoming talk about bee-keeping. He decided that tomorrow he would visit the library and find some books on the subject.

A week after the robbery, Jenny was busy rearranging the roses that Simon had brought for her as a peace offering. A few had died but most had lasted wonderfully well. She had never asked Simon where he had got them. She knew they weren't from the florist because some of the stems were so short she had to put them in a smaller vase.

It didn't matter, she decided. It was the thought that counted, plus she had always loved red roses.

The Attic

The old house was supposed to be haunted. The real estate person hadn't told them that at first; he probably thought it would put them off making an offer. But he needn't have worried. As soon as Nina and Gordon saw the house advertised as a 'handyman's dream', they knew it was the one. For a start, it was in a really nice suburb and they had always decided a good investment would be an old house in a good location which Gordon, who liked to spend time using his carpenter skills renovating, renewing and rebuilding, found too good to refuse. It was a challenge they were both willing to take. Nina was used to living in the middle of a work in progress, so it was no big deal. She knew that when all was finished a profit would be made on the sale. It had worked for the last two houses they had bought, and there was no reason to think this would be any different.

Nina stood in the kitchen with a cup of coffee in her hand looking at the half painted kitchen cupboards. Gordon was at present on his way to the hardware shop to buy more paint and get some bits and pieces for the current job.

She was thinking about the ghost. There had been no evidence of any eerie sounds, thumps in the night, or things moving around of their own accord. Admittedly, there had been a few creaking noises at night as the house settled, especially after a hot day, but this was to be expected in an old house like this.

She wondered where the haunted stories had come from. She had asked the house agent person, who said he didn't know. It was just information which came with the house's history. He had told them it had been a deceased estate which had passed into the hands of auctioneers. Nina resolved that as soon as she could find the time she would go to the local library to see if there was any recorded information about a resident ghost for Hill House, as it was called. In the meantime, she decided it was time to investigate the attic.

They hadn't realised there was an actual attic. There was quite a steep roof, so there would be room, but when they had asked the agent about it, he had passed quickly over the question, remarking that it was just an empty roof space and probably dangerous to enter as there were no floorboards.

The thing was, Nina had noticed that there was a trapdoor in the ceiling over the end of the long hallway near to the outside door, and she had a curious desire to have a look around up there just to satisfy herself. Suddenly making a decision, she went out to the shed and found the stepladder, which she thought would be just high enough for her to reach the ceiling. It took a couple of tries before she got it in just the right position then, feeling quite excited, she climbed up, put her hand underneath the trapdoor and pushed. There was a hinge on the other side and it lifted up quite easily. Nina stood on the top of the ladder and, balancing carefully, manoeuvred the door over to one side until it rested on the inside of the hole. Holding onto both sides of the opening, Nina pushed up until she could see inside. It was dark up there and it took a moment for her eyes to adjust. She looked around. Contrary to what the house agent had said, there were a few floorboards leading over to the side of the room. She could see dust and cobwebs, and just as she was feeling a bit disappointed at finding nothing else, stopped short and gave a little gasp. There, over in the corner, was a big box or chest of some kind. Nothing else, no furniture or anything, just the big chest.

Nina couldn't stop now. She balanced on the top step of the ladder and gradually pushed herself over the edge onto her stomach until she was lying full length on the floor. She lay still for a moment panting a bit, realising that at her age of fifty-two she wasn't as fit as she used to be. Then, getting onto her knees, she finally stood up. She couldn't stand up straight as the roof was sloping too much. So, bending slightly as she made her way gingerly over to the other side of the attic, Nina finally reached the big box. It was like a seaman's chest; she had seen one like it before. There were brass handles, one each end, but there wasn't a padlock or anything. Holding her breath, Nina grabbed hold of the handles, then slowly lifted the lid until it fully opened and came to a stop.

Nina felt prickles over her arms and neck as she peered inside. By now, she was feeling a little bit spooked. There seemed to be tissue paper wrapped around a garment of some kind. Slowly and carefully, she unwrapped the paper from around an emerging dress. It looked discoloured, off-white, but as she gradually pulled it out and held it up, she could see that it had been a quite beautiful long white wedding dress. It had been made for a very small person; the waist was quite tiny. It was made of silk and there was lace, beautiful embroidery, delicate pearl buttons, and a long train attached to the back. Nina gazed at it in wonder. Who on earth could this have belonged to? Why had it been hidden up here?

Questions that made no sense crossed her mind, and Nina suddenly felt cold. She looked around at the open trapdoor and wondered if Gordon had come back and a cool breeze had gone through the house. But all was quiet. Then she froze as something seemed to stir in the dark recesses of the attic. She caught a fleeting glimpse of a quick movement, something indefinable which for a moment seemed to stir the dust. A shiver of fear ran through her body.

That was it. Nina folded the dress back up as quickly as she could and wrapped the tissue paper around it again. Carefully she placed it as she remembered finding it, back into the chest, and closed the lid. She didn't know why, but she knew the dress had to stay where it belonged. She also knew that she had no business being there.

Making her way back to the trapdoor, she lowered herself down until she was sitting on the edge then, gingerly holding on, levered herself back onto the ladder. She closed the trapdoor, climbed back down, then returned the ladder to the shed.

Nina didn't tell Gordon about the attic, or the dress. For one thing he would have made a big deal about her going up there by herself in the first place, and for the second, he refused to believe in ghosts. 'Rubbish,' he'd say. 'There's no such thing. This house is over a hundred years old with wooden floorboards.'

The next time Nina went to town, she called in at the library. Luckily there was a section which dealt with old homes in the area, all in alphabetical order, and there it was: an old black and white photo of their house. Thrilled at her find, she began to read.

THE LEGEND OF HILL HOUSE

Hill House is said to be haunted by the ghost of Sofia Hill, the eighteen-year-old daughter of the Hill family, who were the original owners. Sadly, she was left at the altar on her wedding day when her betrothed was killed on his way to the church. A spooked horse which was pulling the carriage took flight at the sound of a gun fired by a local hoodlum. The carriage overturned, killing the driver and both passengers, one of whom was the young groom, John Storeman, and his best man, Robert Bartel.

The bride to be, Sofia Hill, never recovered from the tragedy and died of a broken heart a year later. She is said to have been heard weeping and pacing the floor at night. However, no real evidence of this has ever been confirmed or documented.

Nina obtained a photocopy of the story from the librarian and then took it home to show Gordon, who said that they should keep quiet about it if they were going to resell the house, as it might put prospective buyers off.

For a while after that, Nina would lay awake at night, listening. Sometimes she thought she heard sounds of quiet weeping coming from above and sometimes when she heard a creak she couldn't help but wonder. But it could all be just house sounds, or rats, or cats outside. Then she stopped worrying about it. But she never ventured into the attic again, and she never told Gordon.

A few months later when all the work was finished, the house went on the market, and they had an open day. An interested young couple walking through asked Nina if there was a room in the roof.

She was quick with her reply. 'No, sorry, just cobwebs and dust, and there's no floorboards, so it's not very safe.'

The Dust Storm

Most people have hope. It may be just a small one – that tomorrow will be fine, that the bus won't be late. Or bigger – like one day having enough money to buy something you need or want. Then even bigger hopes like for world peace and so on. People hope for all manner of things – high hopes to be realised one day. It's hope that keeps you going; otherwise, in my opinion, there doesn't seem to be much point in anything.

Back in the seventies, our family had a farm in outback South Australia and we were living on hope. Just a small one for many people, but a very big one for us. Hope for rain. Never mind hoping for electricity, or a septic tank and a proper toilet instead of the long drop, or a normal stove I didn't have to chop wood for to cook on. Just rain.

It hadn't rained for months. The rainwater tank was nearly empty and the river had almost dried up, rendering the water pump useless. There had been weeks and weeks of searing heat with no respite, and we were exhausted, irritable and ready to go back to the city. It began to look as though this harsh dry land was going to beat us after all.

One Saturday morning in January, the heat was more oppressive than ever. I had just been hanging nappies onto the line, and glanced up at the sky, which seemed to be getting darker. The reason, I soon discovered, was an enormous reddish-brown cloud approaching slowly from the north. It seemed to reach right down to the ground.

I stared unbelievingly at the awesome sight. Something weird was happening and I wished my husband and the boys would hurry home.

At that moment, our old utility heaved itself around the corner and screeched to a stop.

Frank was shouting as he ran towards the house, 'Quickly, inside everybody, close the windows and stuff something under the doors. There's a dust storm coming!'

Even as he spoke, the sun finally became hidden behind a great bank of swirling cloud, turning the day into eerie brown night. The wind strengthened to hurricane force, shrieking and whining over and around us.

Doors and windows shook. We could hear the iron roof rattling and banging on the timber supports, and then an enormous crash as the chimney pot collapsed under the strain. It was at this point that we all dived under the big kitchen table to join Ferguson, our fearless watchdog.

Our two small boys looked white-faced and scared, the baby started yelling in fright and I tried to cover her ears to block out the terrifying noise.

For the next half hour, we huddled together waiting for the storm to pass, and when the wind finally dropped we shakily crawled out from under the table and ventured outside to survey the damage. We could only stand in stunned amazement, staring at the devastation surrounding us.

The neat wood pile had been lifted up and thrown around like matchsticks. Fences were lying broken and tangled up in the barbed wire. The iron copper which I used for the washing had been lifted right off its stand and was tilted drunkenly sideways. Posts, clothes lines and nappies had all disappeared. Sand was piled up against the northern side of the house as though a giant had been trying to bury us all.

Worst of all was the chook house, which had recently been rebuilt. The roof had been torn away, one wall was lying crookedly on the ground, and we made the awful discovery of a pathetic pile of dead chickens half buried under the sand.

Frank called to our sons, 'Come on, you two, there's work to be done.'

As the boys followed behind him to start cleaning up, I heard Kevin say, 'Gee, that was a great storm, wasn't it? Were you scared?'

'Course not,' replied brother Mason. 'Were you?'

'Course not.'

I had to smile as I walked back to the house carrying the baby, who had calmed down now that it was all over, but the smile soon disappeared when I saw the state of the house.

The red sand had seeped into the most unlikely places, through gaps in the walls and roof of the old farmhouse. It was in the cupboards, the beds and clothes. Everywhere had to be cleaned, swept, dusted and washed. It had even managed to creep into the sugar basin inside the kitchen cupboard. The only place I didn't find sandy dust was in the fridge, and for that I said 'thank you' to whoever might have been listening up there!

The heat persisted for another week. I was beginning to hate the bush. It was hard trying to manage with hardly any water, as well as keeping the everyday sand and dust out of the house. There was the endless battle with the old wood stove and its insatiable appetite for mallee stumps, and the terrible fatigue which seemed to have overtaken us all.

I wondered what it was we were trying to prove. Every night someone would say, 'Let's hope it rains tomorrow.'

One day, Mason came running in, shouting with excitement, 'There's a cloud coming. I think it's going to rain. Come on, everybody, COME ON.'

We all ran outside and watched as a big black cloud followed by another one slowly but surely rolled towards us. We could feel a cool breeze coming from the south.

Suddenly a large drop of rain fell, leaving a dent in the sand, then another and another.

'It's raining,' Kevin yelled. 'It's raining, hooray – it's raining.'

And down it came, the blessed, glorious, cool, life-giving rain. We ran around in circles, shouting, laughing and turning our faces upwards so that it could run all over our bodies and cleanse our dusty hair. We kicked off our shoes and ran in the puddles. We could hear the beautiful sound of water trickling into the water tank.

Gradually the rain stopped, but the weather had broken at last. A gentle breeze was coming from the south bringing relief at last from the heat.

That evening we sat outside, blissfully drinking tea that had been made with rainwater instead of boiled-up muddy river water. I found a packet of cake mix I had been keeping for a special occasion, so I threw another lump of wood on the stove and baked a cake.

Out there, the bush was alive with sound. The coming of the rain had revived and renewed all the living things, and with it renewed hope that maybe we would last another year.

The Old Gum Tree

There used to be a big old gum tree in our street. It stood in the front yard of a big old house where there lived a big old lady. Her husband planted that tree fifty years ago when they first moved in, when there were only a few houses in the street, and paddocks over the back. Most of the trees planted around that time have fallen down with age or been chopped up, because they became dangerous. Branches would drop off when there was a bad storm or high winds.

The old gum tree stayed, though. Most people liked it being there. It gave our street character. It provided shade and was a familiar landmark, as was the big old house. It was the oldest building in the street; most of the other old houses had been knocked down to make way for new units and such.

When giving directions to any visitors, we would say, 'Look for the old gum tree' or 'We live just past the old gum tree, outside the old house.' Nobody made a fuss because they knew how the old lady felt about it. Her husband had left her about twenty years ago and run off with a young lady who was neither old nor fat, or so the story goes. No one knows for sure what really happened; he had just disappeared So I suppose that tree reminded her of him. Perhaps it had sentimental value for her, so you could understand that in a way, although if he had left her for a younger woman, you would have thought she wouldn't have wanted any reminders.

Anyway, one day, the council sent around some tree-loppers. I guess they had decided that it was time for the old gum tree to go, but the old lady tied a rope round herself and round the tree and refused to budge. She made such a fuss that someone called the local TV station and they put a piece in the paper with a photograph, making it look as if the council was causing unnecessary stress to this poor old lady, and that it wasn't necessary to cut down a perfectly good tree.

The council left it alone for a bit, but then the inevitable happened. A very strong wind blew up and a big branch fell down on top of some stranger's car, making a big dent and breaking the windscreen. Well, of course he shouldn't have parked under the tree in the first place, but he was furious and threatened to sue the council for negligence, so after that they had no option but to get the tree-loppers back in.

Of course the old lady (whose name by the way was Mrs Higginbottom) made a big fuss again and started shouting and throwing stones at the tree-loppers, who had to call the police. But she had been yelling so much that she fell down and had a heart attack or something and they called an ambulance and took her to hospital.

The tree-loppers got really busy then, and although it took a couple of hours, with all the neighbours standing around gawking, they finally got it done. The problem was the tree roots were so big they had wrapped around the mains water pipe and, what with them digging so deep, somehow the water pipe got broken and a great big gush of water spurted up and there was a dreadful mess. It flooded the road and house and everything else before the water people came and finally mended the pipe.

It was going to be a long time before the old house was fit to live in again, and the old lady never came back. They said she went into a nursing home, which was just as well, as she would have been really upset if she came back and saw that the tree was gone for good. Then when the inspectors had a look at the house they found it was full of termites and past repairing so they had it knocked down and somebody bought the land.

But the interesting thing is that when they started doing the foundations for the new units or whatever, work suddenly stopped. All at once there were police cars in the yard, a big tent was put up over where old tree used to be and you couldn't see what was happening.

Nobody knows what's going on, the police are keeping quiet, and it's a big mystery. Except that today an undertaker's van pulled up and now everyone has their own theories, including me.

Well, it's obvious, isn't it?

Tranquillity

Tranquillity can mean different things to different people. For instance, tranquillity can be found sitting on warm sand at the beach listening to the soothing murmur of the waves, or relaxing in a garden with the smell of new mown grass and the scent of roses hanging in the air.

For Mildred Bartley, it was just what she was doing now. Sitting in her favourite chair with a hot cup of cocoa, two Tim Tams waiting to be munched and a book that she had just started reading. She had turned off the TV after watching a good movie with a happy ending. She liked happy endings. Mildred had turned on the electric blanket and was waiting for the bed to warm up before tucking herself in for the night.

These were small pleasures indeed, but small pleasures as you age are the simple, achievable ones and no less enjoyable than the exuberance of youth, when – in Mildred's opinion – tranquillity was rarely experienced and a word not often used or wanted by the young.

She was reaching for her reading glasses when her peace was suddenly shattered. Someone was banging on the front door.

Mildred froze. Luckily she wasn't holding her cup of cocoa or she most certainly would have dropped it.

She looked at the windows, where the blinds weren't properly closed. If someone had come to the house, then they could see through the window. Struggling to get up quickly, Mildred staggered a bit as she went and quickly pulled all the blind cords tight, then crept quietly towards the front door. A sliver of fear coursed through her being as she remembered she hadn't locked it.

Mildred was almost there when she thought about her walking

stick stowed away behind the door in her bedroom, so she went as fast as she could and found it without turning the lights on. At least, she thought, it's a weapon.

Mildred had been trying to think quickly. The next-door neighbours were away, and the other side was a vacant block. If any of her family wanted to contact her, they would phone. They certainly wouldn't scare her to bits with banging on the door at ten o'clock at night, plus they would call out so that she would know who it was.

She reached in her dressing gown pocket for her mobile phone and then remembered it was on the charger in the kitchen.

The banging started again, louder this time. Mildred recalled someone saying once that if you think there's a stranger knocking at your door, you're on your own and you're feeling threatened, then you should pretend there's a man in the house. Mildred's husband Harry had passed away ten years ago but she still felt his presence, so gathering her breath now and calling out as loud as she could, Mildred shouted, 'Harry, there's someone at the door,'

Then she listened. Perhaps they would go away now. There could hear a shuffling of feet and she wished she had one of those fisheye things fitted into the door so that she could see out. She inched closer, reached out and quickly slid the bolt across. Now they can't get in, she thought, then remembered the back door, but that, she knew, was definitely locked.

Mildred put her ear to the door to listen then jumped back as a man's voice suddenly shouted, 'Come on, Harry, open up. What's going on?'

He sounded angry, and now she was totally confused. Harry? Was this some old friend of Harry's?

There was silence as Mildred thought about what to do. Now that she knew she was safely locked in, she felt a bit better, but there was still no way she was going to open the door to an angry stranger.

'Who are you?' she asked. 'What do you want?'

'None of your business, lady. Just get Harry.'

'Harry's very busy right now,' Mildred said firmly. 'Just tell me who you are and what you want and I'll pass the message on.'

'You don't need to know my name,' he shouted, 'and I'd like to know what's going on. Harry said to be here at ten o'clock to collect the stuff, so unless you open this door right now,' he yelled, 'it'll be curtains for Harry. You tell him that,' and with that he gave another almighty thump on the door.

Mildred was gathering her wits, and the realisation of what might be going on was penetrating the mixed emotions she was experiencing right now.

'I think you've got the wrong house,' she said now, trying to speak calmly, wondering at the same time if this angry stranger was capable of kicking the door down, and whether she should call the police.

There was silence once again, then she realised he was talking to someone else, but there had been no other voice, so he must have been on the phone.

Then he shouted again, 'Is this 66 Maybury Street?'

Mildred detected just a slight confusion mixed in with the belligerent tone. 'No, this is 6B Maybury Close. Maybury Street is the next one. You need to go back up to the main street and turn left. And then it's the next street over,' Mildred explained helpfully.

Again she listened and waited. Then there was a grunt and a loud profanity which made her wince as he gave one last enormous pound on the door. Then she heard the sound of feet quickly retreating.

Mildred gave a big sigh of relief. Phew, she breathed. She went back into the lounge room and over to the mantelpiece on which there was a pretty blue ceramic urn. She gave it a gentle loving pat. 'Well, Harry my love,' she said. 'It looks as though you have a namesake living in our old place at number 66. And business is still booming.' And she smiled.

Even so, she felt a bit rattled when she discovered her cocoa had gone cold, so she zapped it in the microwave, then took it, her Tim Tams on their napkin, and her book and crawled into her now nice warm bed.